Liz Lovelock

MONDAY NIGHT Guy

MY GUY #1

Cover Design by Ben Ellis from Be Designs
Photographer: Lindee Robinson Photography
Models: Travis Bendall & Ali Abela
Edited by Lauren Clarke Editing and Swish Design & Editing
Proofread by Virginia Tesi Carey
Formatted by Tami at Integrity Formatting

www.lizlovelockauthor.com

MONDAY NIGHT

Guy

MY GUY #1

CHAPTER One

amn. I'm late.

My hands clutch a bunch of books tightly to my chest while I sprint and weave my way through bodies along the path to get to my first class.

"Addison!"

I halt in my tracks and turn toward the unfamiliar female voice. Stacey, Parker's girlfriend, is looking directly at me. A puff of air is pushed from my lungs as a large body collides with mine. I fall to the ground, hard. My books clatter on the pavement. Pain throbs in my ass, and a stinging sensation alerts me to a graze on my elbow.

Dammit!

Closing my eyes tightly, I offer up a prayer. *Please don't let anyone have seen that.*

My eyes spring open only to be met with a familiar face and messy longish black hair. Annoyance flares within me. "What the hell, Jimmy?" I yell, as I rub my freshly skinned elbow.

He swiftly lifts his body off the ground, not responding. Instead, he scoops up a few books and walks to where I'm sitting on the ground. He stops at my feet, his massive frame towering over me. "That was all your fault. Next time, don't stop." He chuckles as he turns away.

My face flames. Not from embarrassment, but anger. Jimmy and his merry duo are pains in my ass.

I gather my books off the ground as the sound of laughter fills the air. I glance up, only to see Jimmy now standing with Parker, Dane, and Stacey, who's hanging off her boyfriend's arm. This group has made my college life a living hell. It amazes me how one slip-up made things go from good to bad in the space of a few hours. One night. One kiss.

One huge mistake.

My eyes connect with Parker's, and want burns in his big blues. It's a look I'm all too familiar with when it comes to him. He takes no time in looking me up and down with desire. I don't understand. His girlfriend is standing right beside him. Why does he do that?

Parker, Jimmy, and Dane continue their mirth at something as silly as me falling over. Childish much? How can our college put faith in them to take home the basketball trophy?

After picking up my last textbook, my glare shifts back to the group. Parker's grin makes my hand twitch. I want to slap the smile clear off his face. My first day is starting out perfect. *Not!*

"What are you looking at, Addison? You should take a picture. It'll last longer," Parker jokes, nudging Jimmy with his elbow which results in more snickering.

I quickly avert my eyes. Squaring my shoulders, I try not to let his words affect me, but they do. I liked Parker at one stage, but because I rejected him and stayed with my boyfriend, he plays these stupid games. Messing with my emotions. "Shut it, Parker."

My stomach twists at the familiar growl behind me. I spin around. Hayden stands with his chest pumped out, ready for a fight. His storm gray eyes stare down at me. Chills shoot up my spine. Everything about Hayden *appears* perfect: perfect hair, perfect body, and star quarterback on the football team... but it's not. He's not perfect. Far from it.

I watch his jaw tic—something he does when he's angry or annoyed.

Turning back toward Parker, I notice his stupid grin is still there, but he and his boys have stopped laughing. Heat presses against my back, and I know it's Hayden. "Stop harassing my girlfriend, Parker, or you'll find yourself in a world of hurt," he warns. His tone dangerous.

Hayden's entire demeanor reminds me of a lion claiming a lioness. I know he's not joking.

We've been together since the middle of my freshman year. I'm known as Hayden Masters's girlfriend. He's a junior and recognized by everyone. Since *the incident* at the end of my freshman year, he's become neurotic.

Parker raises his hands in defense. "No harm done."

Hayden takes my arm, gripping it tight enough to leave a mark. He pulls me back, forcing me to stand beside him. When I look up again, I notice Stacey's gone. Hayden's grip tightens, and I try my best to keep a straight face, but his pressure is too much. I screw my face up as his nails press into the tender skin under my arm.

Parker steps toward us. "Let her go, Hayden. Can't you see you're hurting her?" His face is set in stone as his eyes focus on Hayden's grip.

Not wanting more of a spectacle, I step away from Hayden, forcibly pulling my arm out of his grasp. He releases me.

I stare at him. There's annoyance in his glare. Why can't he be the boyfriend he was when we first met? Oh, that's right—*I'm* the one who messed it all up. The one night I had a little too much to drink at an end-of-year party, and I locked lips with Parker. I want to kick myself every time I think about what happened. But Hayden makes sure to use it against me often, making me feel like the worst person in the world. Now, I'm a shell of the girl I once was. I hide what small amount of confidence I still have, and I definitely don't show it around Hayden. Otherwise, I'll get my legs cut out from under me.

I cast my eyes toward the ground, and mumble, "Sorry. I'm late for class. I'll see you later."

Turning, I quickly run away. Throwing a glance back over my shoulder, I catch Hayden walking away from the trio in the opposite direction, but Parker's gaze is firmly on me. An unreadable look I've not seen before rests on his face. His friends don't appear to have noticed since they're still laughing and carrying on like clowns.

I wonder why he stood up for me.

Dread fills my entire body. Hayden will be angry at Parker for telling him what to do.

My relationship with Hayden is toxic. I rub at the hurt still lingering in my arm. The cut on my elbow is nothing. It's the bruises inside that hurt way more.

CHAPTER Two

I arrive at my English class ten minutes late. My heart's still racing. Hayden and his hard stare replay in my mind. It's unnerving. I'm more than a little apprehensive about what our next encounter might entail.

I balance my collection of books under one arm to open the door, only to fumble. When I get control of my books again, I twist the doorknob and push it wide open. All eyes turn and focus on me. I want to curl up and die. How embarrassing.

"Sorry, I'm late. I had—"

The elderly teacher raises her hand, and I snap my mouth shut.

"I don't want your excuses. Find a spare seat."

Eying all the students before me, I nod.

The teacher hands me a syllabus. There's one on every

desk in the room in front of my class members. Some students are smirking, and some seem mad I've disrupted the first class of the year. *Great.*

There are no seats left at the front, where I prefer to sit. One empty spot is open, but when I see whose butt is seated beside it, I want to walk out the way I came in.

Parker Kent. How did he beat me here? And why does he look so relaxed and settled in his chair?

His head is turned down at his book or his phone—I'm not sure. Sucking in a breath, I drag my feet toward the empty spot. I would give anything to be attending another class right now, preferably one this idiot isn't in. I sense his eyes on me but keep my eyes focused on my feet, making no acknowledgment.

I drop my bag to the floor with a thud, which earns me a few more dirty glances. I place the books I've been carting around on the little desk in front of me before plonking myself into the seat.

Before I even have a chance to get set up, Parker leans into my personal bubble. *Uh, hello? Does he not understand personal space?*

His heated breath hits my ear as he whispers, "Hey, Addison. Fancy seeing you here."

Rolling my eyes, I choose to ignore him. Even his voice irritates me.

The teacher continues her first-day-of-class speech. On the board she's scrawled her name in neat cursive writing. *Mrs. Wilson.*

"I will not tolerate tardiness." Her eyes flick to me while I sink farther into my chair. Damn her. I drop my head, fiddling with the hem of my blue shirt. "There are some solo exams, tests, and group projects later in the term, and we'll be choosing those groups when the time comes."

Oh, thank goodness. The last thing I need is for her to announce the person we're working with is the one sitting beside us. I'd give my left leg not to be stuck with Parker. He'd probably make me do all the work anyway, lazy prick.

Mrs. Wilson drones on about what kind of behavior she expects in class and says she only allows extensions on assignments if there's an emergency. I won't be needing those because I'm a high achiever. I've got my head screwed on straight.

I try my hardest to concentrate on what Mrs. Wilson is talking about, but each movement Parker makes stirs up emotions I don't want to feel. He makes me wish I ended things with Hayden, and went with Parker after we'd kissed, but I was afraid. At the same time, I harbor so much guilt about what I'd done, so I stayed. Still, it doesn't help the pull I feel within myself toward Parker. Time's passing ever so slowly. We've only been here for twenty minutes. I need to escape.

I catch movement from the corner of my eye. A neatly folded piece of paper pokes out the side of one of my books. It's from Parker. I don't look his way. Instead, I flick my hair out from behind my ear, allowing it to drop, putting a wall between us.

I take the piece of paper, crunching it in my hand, and throw it in my bag. As it slips inside, my phone vibrates. Peeking up, I search for the teacher... Nope, she's not paying attention. Slightly shifting in my seat so I can remove my cell easily from my pocket, I look at the screen below the small table.

Elsie: Can I swap shifts with you at the café? I need a Thursday night. It'll have to be a permanent thing. I've taken an extra class and will need Monday nights free. Sorry to be a pain.

I quickly reply.

Addison: You're lucky I love you. LOL. Of course I'll swap. So I'm going in tonight?

Elsie's response is lightning speed.

Elsie: Yeah starting at 5 until 9. Thanks again. I'll see you later back at the dorm. Love you, sweet cheeks.

I grin, shaking my head at my nickname. Sweet cheeks.

Usually, I work Thursday nights and Saturday mornings, then throw in the occasional shift here and there when I'm needed and can do it. It works well. Jen, the owner, of the café we both work at, only gives jobs to the students. She's an excellent boss. I love working with her.

"Are you ignoring me?" Parker's low voice startles me. I jump, my cell dropping with a loud clunk on the floor. Oh, my goodness. My hands rub down my face.

"What was that?" The teacher looks out over the students. No one responds. I put my head down, hoping no one points or looks in my direction. "I won't stand for poor behavior," she grumbles.

I flick an angry scowl to Parker. His eyes widen as he bites his lip, appearing to hold back laughter. *Gah! Why does he have to be in this class?*

There's a stillness to the room. Turning back toward the board, Mrs. Wilson makes more notes. I lean over, collecting my phone from the floor while muttering under my breath at the idiot beside me.

"Good going, Addison," Parker whispers.

I hear his held back laughter and this time, catch a whiff of his minty breath. He's so close—too close. His warmth causes the side of me to tingle from head to toe.

I'm 100 percent sure if I turned toward him, our lips would connect. I don't move.

"That will be all for today," Mrs. Wilson announces. *Oh, thank you!*

Standing up, I slip my backpack onto my shoulders and scoop up the remainder of my stuff. My legs pump it, attempting to get out of there quickly while trying to put some distance between myself and Parker. I reach the door, swinging my head around, and glance back.

Parker's stare follows me out of the room.

CHAPTER
Three

My mouth waters as I pull the blueberry muffin from the showcase, placing it on a plate ready to be devoured. Break time.

Tonight has been pretty quiet. I suppose most people don't need their caffeine hits yet. Wait a few more weeks when people are trying to cram for exams and assignments. Then they'll be demanding coffee in an IV.

Sliding on to the stool behind the counter, I raise the muffin to my lips, taking a bite. It tastes good, I almost moan. Jen's cooking is to-die-for. I pick up my cell from the counter and aimlessly scroll through messages and apps, wondering if I need them, when my phone rings. Devon's name appears on the screen.

With a swipe of my finger, I answer, "What's up, little bro?"

Devon calls every Monday at eight-thirty on the dot.

It's become a part of his routine since I moved out onto campus. I didn't have the heart to cancel on him tonight. I'd mentioned to Jen when I first arrived he'd call, for his peace of mind. I need to let him know I'm okay and tell him about my day.

Jen was very understanding. Devon has autism and can function well amongst others, but he has to follow the routine he's made for himself to be able to withstand going to school and out in public.

"Hey, Addy." I hear the familiar tapping he does on the speaker every time we talk on the phone. "How was your first day back?"

"It's been good. Getting settled. How was yours?"

Tap, tap, tap. "Some boys weren't very nice to me, but I ignored them." Devon must be nervous. His voice trembles more than usual. Also, the tapping is more consistent.

Sitting up a little straighter on my chair, I bristle. With a clench of my fist, I shelve wanting to march into his school tomorrow and do some ass whooping. "What happened? Did you tell Mom and Dad?"

Devon sighs. *Tap, tap, tap.* "Yes. Yes, I did, Addy."

"Well, what did they do?" I take another bite of my muffin as I wait for his answer.

"Mom says she'll talk to the school tomorrow." He taps again.

Rolling my eyes, I try to control my anger and frustration. I love Mom and Dad dearly, but sometimes they become so caught up in themselves, each other, and their work, that they don't support Devon like I wish they would.

I place my muffin down, step up off the stool and start

pacing. "If she doesn't, Devon, call me, and I'll talk to Mom."

"It's fine, Addy. I'm all right. Tommy's here. We're doing our homework."

I hear shuffling in the background, and Tommy's familiar voice shouts "hello" down the phone line.

I laugh. "Okay then. Tell Tommy I said hey, and make sure you talk to Mom again. I'm going to call her as well." We say our goodbyes.

As I put my cell on the bench, the bell chimes and the café door swings open. I glance up, smiling, ready to greet the customer.

My smile drops off my face, and a scowl draws down in its place.

"Hey, Addison. Fancy seeing you here." Parker grins, strutting up to the counter, pressing one of his palms on the bench as he leans forward.

Parker has a bright orange basketball tucked under his tattooed arm, and a sports bag slung over his shoulder. His toned biceps are out on display and glisten with a sheen of sweat. He looks damn fine in his training gear— a bright red basketball singlet, and black sports shorts.

Clenching my jaw together, I attempt to control my irritation. I plaster a fake smile on my face. "What do you want?"

I'm no good with niceties. He irks me, yet, there's this pull toward him.

He lifts his bag, pushing it onto the counter, knocking my plate and muffin to the floor. The plate smashes as it hits the tiles.

"Dammit," I yell, jumping back.

Parker races around the counter. "I'm so sorry,

Addison." He bends down and starts collecting the larger pieces.

"Seriously. What is your problem?" I blurt out. "First, I'm bowled over by your jerk of a friend, then you made it hard for me to focus in English, and now you're here in my workplace, ruining my muffin and destroying things." My hands gesture to the mess at my feet and by the end of my rant, I'm yelling and puffed.

Finally, I glance down at him. He's stopped what he was doing and is staring up at me. His eyebrows are raised high in shock, I think.

Jen's face appears in the doorway. She looks between Parker and me. "Ahh… is everything okay?" Her gaze falls on the smashed plate scattered over the floor.

"Yeah, sorry. I'll get this cleared up, Jen."

She nods and disappears out back again.

I turn my attention back to Parker. A grin slowly spreads across his features. I want to slap it right off his smug face.

"Wow, Addison." He rises to his full height, about a foot taller than my five-foot frame. "There's the girl I remember from last year. I thought you'd become this meek little mouse. Now your true colors have come out once again."

My hands go to my hips while I frown at him. "What's that supposed to mean?"

"You've changed," he states.

Where's he going with this? "Shut up, Parker. Leave it. Tell me what you want so I can get you out of my way."

He spins around, struts to the fridge, grabs a sports energy drink, and comes back, placing it on the counter. He pulls some cash out of his bag and hands it to me.

With shaky hands, I ring up the purchase. *Why the hell are my hands shaking?*

It must be the incident of the plate. Yep, that's what I'll put it down to.

Things between us remain silent. I press my lips together, biting my tongue so as not to say something I might regret later. Although, I've already given him a mouthful, and it didn't seem to faze him a single bit.

"No need to be nervous, little mouse. It's only me," he teases.

I thrust his change into his open palm, trying hard not to make contact. His hand closes as I drop the money in. He holds my hand for a brief moment. I look at him. His thumb grazes my fingers. My stomach twists.

What's this game he's playing?

"Did you read my note?" He throws his bag back over his shoulder and heads toward the door, not giving me a chance to reply. "See you in class, little mouse."

Then he's gone, and I'm left cleaning up the disaster.

I step out of the café after saying goodbye to Jen, the still night air surrounding me. It's peaceful, in a way. I think going to shoot some hoops would take the edge off my mixed up emotions I've been feeling all day. Grabbing my cell from my pocket, I groan. It's as if a bucket of ice-cold water has been poured over my body. Great. Just what I need to deal with tonight. No shooting hoops for me now.

Hayden: We need to talk. Call me.

Deciding not to poke the bear, I put my cell away. I'll go see him instead and get his drama over with.

Hayden and some other football players live in a house across from campus. Turning away from the path back to my dorm, I walk toward the road out front of the college.

I wonder what Parker's deal is. Stopping abruptly, I drop my bag to the ground with a thud. Rifling through my backpack, I pull out book after book, looking for the tiny crumbled piece of paper I threw in amongst the chaos of my bag. When the contents are splayed across the pavement, I find the note Parker left in my book right in the bottom of my backpack.

"Always the way," I murmur, and start shoving everything back into the tiny space. So many damn books. I stop under the streetlight and unfold the crumpled piece of paper.

I'm more confused after opening it. There's a phone number. It would have to be Parker's. It must be some stupid joke he and his trio are playing on me, to see if I call or message. *Not going to happen, buddy.* I thrust it into my jeans pocket and continue on.

When I arrive at the crossing, I see the house. Lights are on, and there are a number of cars out front. *Perfect— they must be having a party.*

The idea of going back to my dorm is very appealing right now. I don't want to worry about Hayden and his issues tonight. Yet, here I am, seeking him out to fix the problem he apparently has.

I stand in front of the house. The front door is wide open with people coming in and out. There's laughter and loud talking amongst a group of students on the front lawn. The music blares from inside the house. I'm not sure how the neighbors feel about all this racket. If I was next door, I'd be unhappy with the noise level.

I don't want to do this. I could be back at my dorm,

getting ready for bed. Instead, I'm preparing myself to confront an unhappy Hayden. *Time to face the music.*

I walk toward the step, my stomach a bundle of anxious knots. I don't want to make a scene, but I don't want to ignore his request either. Ignoring Hayden means more bruises, and that's not something I can handle.

I step through the doorway. The stench of beer assaults my nose. The living room and hallway are jam-packed with bodies. My eyes find a group of my older sister's giggling sorority sisters. I look around and see no sign of her, though I'm sure she's found someone to take her back to their room for the night. Ella's a bitch. We do not get along at all.

A large body stumbles into me. I fall forward, and flashbacks of today's incident flick through my mind. Within seconds, two large muscular arms scoop around my waist, steadying me. Looking up, I'm gifted with a smile from Hayden's friend, Jase. He's a decent guy, one of the few around these days.

"Oh, sorry," Jase says as I steady myself.

"Thanks, Jase. That could have ended badly." I give a hesitant giggle. Straightening, I adjust the weight in my backpack.

He steps away, very alert. His focus darts around the room. There's panic in his wide blue eyes. He doesn't appear to want to meet my gaze. Why?

He stops and looks at me, finally. "Oh, Addy, how are you? Didn't realize it was you. Does Hayden know you're here?" He does another sweep around the room.

I follow his gaze, trying to spot what he might be trying to see. "I'm good, thanks. No, he doesn't know. Have you seen him?"

Jase stops and gives me a hesitant headshake to say no.

The typically chatty guy becomes a speechless mute. *What's got him shaken?*

I shrug, pushing my way past him. "Not a problem. I'll go check his room."

Jase's hand whips out, gripping my arm, stopping me. His eyes turn sad. His usual glistening blues are now dull. *Something's going on—something he doesn't want me to see or know about.*

"Don't go up there, Addy," he warns, a seriousness in his tone.

I shake my head. *Is Hayden cheating on me?*

"What's going on?" I grit out slowly, pulling myself from his hold. Little by little, I back away. He tries to take my hand to stop me, but I dodge him and sprint through an open space and up the stairs.

I march with purpose to the familiar room I've spent many nights in. Not bothering to knock, I throw the door open. It bangs against the wall. Once my gaze adjusts to the dimness of the room, naked bodies move before me. I'm not sure what possessess me, but I erupt in laughter.

What the actual hell?

CHAPTER
Four

*L*aughter bubbles out of me until tears are flowing down my cheeks. Oh goodness, what's wrong with me? Perhaps I've completely lost the plot. Two familiar stunned faces stare back at me.

"I can't believe this." I purse my lips tightly together, clearing my throat in an attempt to settle myself, but it becomes too much. The hilarity of this moment keeps the laughter coming until my stomach begins to hurt. People are going to think I'm crazy, I'm sure of it.

"Damn, are you okay, Addison?" Jase stands beside me. His furrowed brow tells me he's unsure about my reaction to my boyfriend cheating on me, with Parker's girlfriend, Stacey.

What would Parker think if he were here witnessing this?

Stacey is a sophomore, same as me, and has let every guy she meets into her pants. Yet, for some stupid reason, she fought hard to date Parker. She had to have him. He's the basketball captain and popular, which suits her style. I guess she's had enough of him. Time to move on and ruin someone else's relationship in the process. I'm thankful to her, even though she's a slut.

I realize I haven't answered Jase. My hands grip my now sore ribs, and I reply, "Sure why not? My boyfriend is sleeping with someone else's girlfriend," I yell, holding back more fits of giggles.

Gosh, am I broken?

I watch their naked asses scurry out of bed, pulling their clothes on one piece at a time. Stacey is, of course, the first dressed, tugging a short floral green and white flowing dress over her head. It falls over her slender body perfectly. I hate her for looking so damn good. Of course, she has no underwear on. *Damn. She came prepared.*

Jase shifts his body to stand behind me. His hands grip my shoulders. I'm not sure if he's trying to comfort me or hold me back. Heck, I'm not even sure how I'm feeling right now. Everything inside me is a mess, like a jumbled up Rubik's cube. All the colors spread around the cube in disarray.

Stacey steps into the doorway, while Jase's fingers tighten. I step up to her, ignoring the hand attempting to stop me. It's a good thing we're pretty much the same height—I'm maybe a tiny bit taller when I raise myself up. "Thank you for saving me from continuing what could have been the biggest mistake of my life," I begin sarcastically, but now serious. "Now, be sure to hurry home and tell *your* boyfriend, because if you don't, I'm sure there are plenty of little birdies here tonight who might do it," I threaten without a hint of humor in my voice.

Stacey doesn't look fazed. In fact she has a good resting bitch face. *Does she even care for Parker?* I don't think so. Her eyes follow the length of my body, her lips plumped out in a duck-lip pose. A disapproving glint is in her stare. A snarl of a smile swipes across her face. There's pure evil in this girl.

She takes a step closer to me. With venom in her voice, she says, "Listen here, bitch." Her chest presses against my own. I don't back down. "No one will ever believe *a nobody* like you." Her finger waves in my face as her fiery glare searches me up and down again. Her hands come up, and she places her filthy mitts on my shoulders, giving me a shove out of her way.

I clench my fist, ready to go at her for touching me when something stops me—or, should I say, someone. Looking over, my stomach plummets. *Parker.*

Parker stands at the top of the stairs. He's still in the same outfit he was in earlier. *Damn, those arms.* I give my head a slight shake, removing the thought. Parker's face is red with anger. Stacey looks at me, horrified, then back to Parker. It all plays out in front of me, like a bad movie. I look around at the many faces assembled around us in the hall. It appears we've gathered quite an audience. I spot sight of my sister. She, for some strange reason, gives me a sympathetic half grin. I shrug in return. *Was this thing with Stacey happening long before I found out? Did Ella know?*

Parker bolts down the stairs.

"Parker, baby, please," Stacey begs, running after him. *Poor guy.* I can't think about his feelings right now, though; I've got my own to worry about.

I sense Hayden standing beside me, watching Stacey chase Parker. I turn and face him. He's smiling—he's actually freaking smiling. My blood boils with rage so intense it makes me want to hurl myself at him and cause him severe pain.

He reaches for me, and I lift my foot, ready to step away from him, but Jase yanks me away. He comes around in front of me, his shoulders squared and his face hard. Hayden flicks his now angry glare on Jase, as though he's ready to take a swing at him for stopping him from touching me. Hayden fixes his stare back on me. Opening his arms, I stare at him, gobsmacked. *Does he expect me to leap into them?* I think he has another thing coming.

"Addy, baby," he coos, as if I didn't spring him having sex with Stacey.

I clench my fists, wanting to punch him in his pretty face, suddenly finding the strength I had before he squeezed the life and fight out of me. I should have ended this earlier, it's my fault for letting it go on this long. Never again will I let this happen. I step around Jase, and jab my finger into Hayden's chest. "Don't 'baby' me, you dick. It's over."

Jase stands close, his focus on Hayden's every move. I suppose he knows the exact type of person Hayden is, they do spend time together being on the football team together. I thought I was the only one.

Hayden's hand lashes out. He clasps my arm tightly in his grip. I open and close my hand ready to swing, only another body jumps in front of me, stopping my actions. Before I can register what's going on, Jase has pulled me away from the fight that's erupted between Parker and Hayden. I didn't even see Parker return.

Yelling from other party-goers fills the hall. "Fight, fight, fight," they chant in sequence.

Jase's large body surrounds me, protecting me. I peek around him and catch Parker taking another swing at

Hayden. It's bittersweet revenge. I grin, pleased with the outcome. I hope Parker makes him bleed.

Guys rush out from nowhere, pulling Hayden and Parker apart. There's blood pouring from Hayden's mouth and a bright red spot on his cheek. It looks angry. *Good.* I'm sure a nice bruise will show up there. I burst out laughing again and receive a death stare from Hayden.

Somewhat quickly, I compose myself by shifting my gaze to Parker, who's panting heavily. Jimmy and Dane grip his arms. The trio is all together.

Parker shrugs off his boys. Pointing a hateful finger toward Hayden, he threatens, "Stay out of my way, Masters, or you'll have two black eyes and no teeth."

Hayden spits some blood out. *Why did he do that?* Gosh, he's stupid. "Oh, please, Kent. You knew what you were getting into when you started dating her." Hayden laughs, wiping away some more blood.

"You're just as bad as she is. Don't think I don't know about all the other girls, including your girlfriend's sister."

Everything stops.

I feel a heap of stares shift in my direction.

The urge to run is powerful.

I don't find the strength to lift my lead-weight feet. It's as though I've received a knife jab to the heart, and it was given a twist simply for the heck of it.

Slowly, I register what Parker's said. No, it couldn't be. *Would she do something so horrible to me?* My head swings to where I saw Ella earlier, and her mouth is hanging open.

My eyes begin to burn. Tears form. Aren't I the fool?

Everything around me blurs. I need to get out of here. Fast.

Before I know it, I'm being guided down the stairs by

Jase and out the front door onto the lawn. I suck in the night air, attempting to hold back the flood of tears which are on the verge of humiliating me some more.

A muffled voice pulls me from my weird state. Jase is in my face. "Addison, are you okay?" His hands grip my arms. "Addison?" He shakes me a little.

I close my eyes briefly then reopen them. There's sadness in his expression. Sadness for me? He releases me, then brushes a hand through his messy blond hair.

I should have known my sister would do anything to hurt me.

I hate her.

She's nothing to me.

Taking another short breath, I respond, "I'm fine. I'm going to go now." Numbly, my legs start to shuffle toward campus.

"Do you want me to walk you back?" he offers.

"I'll take her." Twisting toward the voice, I see it's Parker. I catch a glimpse of a shiner on his cheek, although there's no blood—unlike Hayden.

I smile. Seeing Hayden hurt makes me feel a little better.

A pang of hurt shoots through me. It's Parker who embarrassed me more by announcing my sister's infidelity.

I shake my head. "No, I'll be all right. I need to clear my head." I don't particularly want company, and especially not his.

Parker scoffs. "Don't argue with me, little mouse. Let's go." He takes my arm tenderly, guiding me away from the house of horrors.

I pull out of his grip, walk back to Jase, and wrap my

arms around him. "Thanks for looking out for me tonight."

"Anytime," he whispers into my hair, which hangs loose. The strong scent of his spicy aftershave hits me.

I step back. "Thanks again," I repeat before leaving with the waiting Parker.

Things between us are silent, so I look around. "Where's Stacey?"

"Who cares?"

More silence, apart from our shoes crunching on the pavement. In my head, I attempt to sift through the events of the evening. If I'd called Hayden like he'd wanted me to, this wouldn't have happened, and I'd still be dating him. I give a sideways glance to Parker, who usually isn't this quiet.

"Are you all right?" I ask, unsure of what else to say. We don't have a good track record of conversations.

Parker bursts out laughing. I look at him, horrified, but can't help but do the same. His laugh is infectious. He's as messed up as me. "Damn, little mouse, you have some bite." He chuckles. I shrug and give a small grin. "Thanks. You give a good right hook."

Our laughter fills the night, and it's pleasant.

"I'll admit, but only to you… it felt incredible causing him pain. Usually, I'm a lover, not a fighter, but he deserved every punch in the face he received."

I catch him clenching his fists again. Reaching out, I touch his bare arm. Whoa, it's like a rock, or is he tensing for my benefit? "Thanks for being the fighter tonight. I was ready to hit Hayden myself before you stepped in."

He stops walking and looks at me, his eyebrows raised in question. "You… you were going to hit him? I would have paid money to see you take a swing." A half grin appears on his face as he continues walking.

It's then I notice a different side of him. Yes, he can be a complete dick, but he has another more relatable, easy-to-talk-to side. I've never had the chance to see this before. After our encounter last year there wasn't much talking happening.

"Hey, just because I'm a girl doesn't mean I can't give a good swing if I need to," I say. He gives me a sideways glance which says, 'whatever you say.' "I do karate and kickboxing. I could probably drop you on your ass if I needed to."

"Do it," he challenges.

Is he joking?

I stop walking. He steps in front of me, ready and waiting.

I toss the idea around in my head. I can drop him, and when I do will laugh my ass off. I slide my bag off my back, placing it on the ground. Parker stands before me. His arms are wide open, waiting, challenging me. A mischievous grin is on his cute face.

CHAPTER
Five

"Come on, little mouse, do it," he goads, stepping on to the lawn beside the pavement. His mouth opens, as though he's about to speak, but he doesn't get a chance to finish his sentence. I snatch his wrist, twist myself into his firm body, and pull his arm over my shoulder. I bend my torso, flipping him over my hunched back. Parker lands flat on his back, looking up at me. A stunned look of admiration is on his face.

"I think I love you," he jokes, still lying there in front of my feet.

"Don't get ahead of yourself. You're still a jerk."

Parker clutches his hand over his chest as if I've offended him. "Ouch. Stab to the heart. Can a heart break twice in one night?"

I know it's meant to be a joke, but I find myself pondering his question. "Well, after finding my boyfriend with your girlfriend, I pissed myself laughing. I think my heart hurt more finding out about my sister and Hayden." I give him a pointed stare, making sure he knows I'm not happy with how he blurted that little fact out.

Parker sits up, resting his arms on his knees, turning to face me. His shoulders slump. "I'm sorry. I was so damn angry."

"You and me both." I laugh nervously. I bend over and collect my bag, throwing it over my shoulders. Parker jumps effortlessly to his feet, like a ninja. He'd have to have smooth moves, playing basketball. *Mental note: watch one of his games this year.*

I love sports, but I don't usually go to the big games unless the girls or Devon want to go. Hayden didn't like me going to watch him when he'd play, I still went, occasionally. He told me once I put him off. Now I think about it, it was probably his way of getting into other girls' pants, since I wasn't there. *What a bag of dicks.*

Cars fill the streets. A few students are walking around.

"You all right?" Parker gently touches my arm. A prickling sensation spreads through me. *Weird.*

I shrug. "Honestly, I don't know. Are you?"

"Yeah. I should have known what I was getting myself into."

I nod, agreeing with him.

"What?" he asks, his tone startling me. I hadn't realized he was paying so much attention to me. My facial expression must have given away more than I realized. "What?" I repeat, trying to play dumb.

"Your face just then was like a 'you should have known, all right' type of expression." He throws his arm over my shoulders, adding to the weight I'm already lugging around.

I scoff. "Yeah, you should have known. Everyone knows the kind of girl Stacey is."

Parker's silent for a moment as though pondering my statement. "How did *you* not know about Hayden then?"

Whoa, sucker punch to the stomach.

I pull away from his touch and stop, eyeballing him with daggers. Anger flares within me, and I don't hold back. My index finger jabs him hard in the chest. "Just because you got hurt tonight, you decided to take another stab at Hayden, and in turn, took a giant stab at me. Screw you, Parker."

I storm off. How dare he? Yes, perhaps I should have known better, but I didn't deserve things to be outed the way they were. Just when I was beginning to see something different in Parker, he went and tossed it back in my face. Damn, I want to punch something. I feel the urge to run, to clear my head.

"Addison! Wait up," Parker calls.

I ignore the loser and run faster. It doesn't take long for him to catch me at the gates of the college campus. He attempts to grab my arm. I pull it away. I stop, glaring at him.

"Sorry," he says, though I'm not sure it was very heartfelt.

"Yeah, you should be. Just leave me alone, Parker." My words crack with high emotion. Turning away from him, I head toward my dorm, not looking back, and this time Parker doesn't follow. Tears rush down my face, and they don't stop even when I arrive back at my room. Thankfully, the girls aren't here. Wishing today didn't happen, I collapse on my bed, smothering a pillow to my face. I also wish I'd never met Hayden Masters, and that Ella didn't exist.

I'll never date a boy like Hayden again. I'm done with guys like him.

"What happened to you last night?" A body slams on top of me, crushing me farther into my mattress. *Elsie.*

"Oh, get off me," I grumble. I shuffle out from under her, my face still buried in my bed. Her body weight shifts off mine slowly. I don't want to face the aftermath of last night.

"So… did you hear Parker beat up your boyfriend last night?" Her tone is more than a little casual. *News travels fast around here.* I roll over and peek out from under my blankets, only my eyes showing. Elsie's now sitting up, and she's wearing her rainbow unicorn pajamas. Her hair is a tangled, golden–brown mess, and it's as though she's just leaped from her bed. Her cell phone is clutched in her hand, and she's watching something.

"What time is it?" I groan, avoiding her topic of conversation.

"Six-thirty."

I bolt upright. She receives my death stare. "Why are you waking me up now?" I slam my body back down and cover my head, ready and hoping for sleep. "Go away," I mumble.

Elsie doesn't budge. "Why won't you answer my question?"

"What question?" I exhale, throwing the blanket off me, knowing exactly what she's talking about. I don't have any desire to relive last night's events. The embarrassment of it all was enough for me.

Elsie turns toward me, propping her leg up on the bed. "Parker and Hayden… fight?" She raises her eyebrows.

Rolling my eyes I respond, "How do you know?" I sigh dramatically, rubbing my hands down my face.

Elsie hands me her phone. "Here."

On the screen, there's a video ready for me to watch. I hit play, and my mouth hangs open in shock. The video is a blow-by-blow of what happened last night. From the moment Stacey ran after Parker, to when Parker and Hayden got into it. This is terrible. It's going to be the gossip of the day. Just what I need.

"Oh, my goodness. Why?" I cry out loudly. I look back up at Elsie, who's watching me intently. "How could this have happened? Do you know what happened before this?" I shake her phone at her, then toss it away from me as though I'll catch some sort of disease just by its close proximity.

She shakes her head.

"Well, I opened the door to Hayden bumping around in the sheets with Stacey, the tramp." My voice grows louder and more agitated with each spoken word. The annoyance from last night slowly returns to a crescendo.

"What?" Elsie leaps off the bed, her face turning a different shade of red. A flame of rage lights behind her eyes. "Oh, wait until I see him again," she grits out through clenched teeth.

Her feet hit the carpeted floor hard as she paces the length of our bedroom.

There are four girls in this shared dorm, and I share a room with Elsie. There are two beds against the cream-colored walls, and desks at the end of our beds. We both have our own nightstand beside us. It's nothing fancy, but it is home.

Elsie continues to stomp around our room. I say nothing. Last night was messed up. My sister. Hayden. Parker and his... whatever it was. I shake away the thoughts of how dropping Parker to the ground made me feel, and the weird sensation I got when he touched me. *He's a jerk.*

Unexpectedly, my door flies open and in waltzes Willow and Jane. *Seriously? Let's have a party.*

"Oh, my goodness, what do you all want? Can't a girl sleep-in?" I ask.

Willow and Jane stare at me. Their jaws drop, as if they're planning to catch flies with their open traps. Their cell phones are in their hands also.

Thank you, social media, for ruining my day.

I'm not sure if my sister will want to talk about what came to light last night. A small part of me wishes that, as my sister, she wouldn't have slept with my boyfriend in the first place. If I found out one of my friend's partners were cheating, I'd march straight to my friend and tell her.

With everyone now crammed into Elsie and my room, the chatter starts all over again.

"What happened with Hayden last night?" Willow begins the line of questioning.

It's Jane's turn next. "Stacey's such a bitch. I don't know what Parker was thinking when he started dating her. Everyone knows she will sleep with anyone." She shakes her head in disgust.

Bring on the fiery Elsie yet again. "Hayden's a dead man walking. What a dick."

The cursing and slandering of Hayden and Stacey gets thrown back and forth between the three of them. It's like watching a game of hot potato. Elsie has a turn, then throws the potato to Willow, who spews her hatred for Hayden. We can't forget Jane now, as it's tossed back to her.

Jane turns to me, her blonde hair in a messy bun sitting perfectly on top of her head. She perches on the edge of

Elsie's bed across from me. "How could he do this to you?"

Three faces stare at me, waiting for I-don't-know-what.

"He's a douchebag. That's how." Willow sits beside me, wrapping her arm around my shoulders, comforting me.

I'm grateful the girls weren't here last night when I arrived home in tears. I think they would have gone in search of Hayden and castrated him.

My cell comes to life beside my bed with a message. Taking a peek at it, I groan when I see Hayden's name on the screen. Willow releases me to look at the lit screen, and she scoffs distastefully.

"Who's it from?" Elsie jumps off the bed and leaps for my phone before I get a chance to take it and even read the message. She groans. "Really? This dick wants to start this now? I mean, I'm your friend, and I have every right to wake you up. This guy…" She points at my cell to the now opened message. "Hayden better not give you hell, or he'll receive it from me."

These girls—I love them fiercely, even though they can be a handful sometimes. Leaning toward Elsie, I snatch my cell back. "Thanks for all the support, girls. Ya know I love your enthusiasm. I need it. How about y'all keep an ear out for some parties this weekend? I'm in desperate need for some time out with my girls."

They all leap on me, giving me a massive bear hug. Laughter ripples around the room. *How can I ever feel down with this group of friends surrounding me?*

After more words of encouragement and bad-assery from my band of crazy, I finally take a moment to read Hayden's message—which has now transformed into four messages in thirty minutes.

Today's going to be a long one.

CHAPTER

Six

O pening the first text, I grit my teeth together.

Hayden: I'm so sorry, Addy. Please forgive me.

Hayden: It was a dumb mistake. I want you back.

Hayden: I promise to be different. I can change.

Hayden: It was all your sister. She instigated it.

My blood simmers with fury at his last message. *What does he take me for? An idiot?*

Standing from my bed, I pace the floor. With each step, I have the urge to run. Going to my cupboard, I pull out my black tights and a black and pink tank top. Pulling them on, followed by my sneakers, I'm out the door before any of the girls have a chance to ask where I'm going.

I load up my running playlist and put my headphones

in. "Novocaine" by Fall Out Boy belts away. Its rhythm pours through my body.

As soon as I'm out of my building, the morning sun kisses my skin. Its warmth is welcoming. Lately, the days haven't been too hot; instead, there's a lovely fall feel. I run between the old-style buildings of River Valley College, which have been in this town for years.

Heading toward the campus gates and passing by the unopened café, I clear my head of the last twenty-four hours, if only for a moment. I find my pace and keep to the beat of my music.

My thoughts trace back to last night no matter how much I try to forget. I was blind to the fact something was going on. I'm so stupid.

Then there's Ella. She hasn't even tried to contact me. *How can she call herself my sister?*

What kind of sister would hurt their own flesh and blood? A bitch—that's the kind.

I don't want her apology, even though she hasn't offered it. In fact, I don't want anything more to do with her.

My pace quickens, and my breathing becomes erratic. Sucking in some long, hard breaths, I set myself back in the right breathing pattern. *In through the nose, out through the mouth.*

I focus on my feet, one moving in front of the other on the speckled pavement below.

Oomph.

I collide with a sweaty bare chest. I stumble back, holding my arms away from me as they are now filthy, covered in someone else's sweat. Eww.

"What the heck?" I swipe the sweat away on my clothes, wishing for a shower right about now.

Glancing up, I'm staring into the familiar blue eyes of Parker Kent. I pull my earbuds out and place my hands on my hips, I frown at him. His stare isn't trained on me now, though, he watches a car go past on the street. "Great. Just what I need this morning. I'm punished by running into one of the few people I don't wish to see or speak to." I groan with displeasure.

Parker says nothing while panting hard, and my eyes rake over his half-naked, tattoo-covered, body while it glistens from the sunlight hitting his sweaty, yet very well-defined, sculpted muscles. The delicious V muscle he has going on above his shorts, is to-die-for. I had no idea he had this much ink on his skin. I want to reach out and touch the fine lines of each image.

His head hangs low. Ever so slowly, he pulls the earbuds from his ears and looks up at me.

"Sorry, were you saying something?" He swipes his hand over his face.

I watch every move he makes, his muscles flexing and rotating. My stomach tightens, and tiny butterflies take flight. I shake my head clear of the no-go zone. "I said, watch where you're going next time."

He shrugs, unfazed. "Sorry. Was caught up in my running and lost track of things. Other people included." He doesn't look at me. Apparently, his cell is more interesting.

I place my earbuds back in my ears, and I'm about to keep running when a light touch on my arm stops me. Flicking my head up, I realize Parker's trying to speak to me.

Pressing pause on my music, I ask, "What did you say?"

Parker holds his phone out to me.

I look down at the video. "I've already seen it."

Parker takes his cell and slides it into his pocket. "Oh, you have, have you?"

I nod. *Where's he going with this?*

He shuffles his feet before speaking. "How are you this morning? Still hating me?"

My eyebrows shoot up in surprise. Parker's watching me, a gentleness swirls in his gaze. Is he being genuine? I never know how to take him. The Parker I knew a year ago is the same one who stands before me, but this one, he has a much bigger ego. More girls chase him these days, and compared to those girls, I'm nothing. I'm one of the tiniest fish in the grand ocean.

Clearing my tight throat, I answer, "You're a jerk. What more can I say? I'll survive this stupid Hayden stuff."

Parker nods, gifting me with a devious grin. "Have you heard from Hayden or your sister?"

"I don't see how me and my sister are any of your business." *Does he not realize I'm not happy with him?*

"Stacey's tried to call a bunch of times. Even showed up at my house." He sighs with clear frustration.

"I can't believe she won't leave you alone." I wave my arms about like a lunatic. "Well, Hayden says it was my sister's fault. He wants me back." I release an exasperated puff of air at the thought. Going back to him would be like giving myself a sentence. *I sentence you to a life of misery.* No thanks.

Parker startles me by stepping closer, wrapping his arms around my body. My laughter stops. I don't budge in his grip. Even though he may be covered in sweat beads, he still smells good. Tantalizing, even.

"Umm… are you okay?" I still haven't managed to wrap my head around how super fine his half-naked body is. My heart thrums with excitement. I want to wrap my arms around him. My head screams at me. *Retreat. Retreat.* What's Parker doing?

He stands upright, releasing me. "Thanks for making me laugh. Sometimes we need someone to lighten our loads, and you helped me today."

I point to myself. "Me? I don't think I did much. In fact, I'm still a little pissed at you." I laugh nervously.

Parker shrugs.

Beside us, more cars move about the streets. The sun's higher in the sky. I quickly glance at my cell, gripped tightly in my hand. "Well, I have to go, or I'll be late again for another class."

"I had nothing to do with Jimmy and his stupidness yesterday."

"I don't care. What got to me was how you all stood around and watched me scramble for my books, while I looked like a fool. I don't get you, Parker. It's like there are two sides to you. The jerk, who makes more appearances than he should, and then there's this…" I gesture to him. "I don't even know what to call this side of you yet."

Parker doesn't seem too pleased with my description of his double personality. He crosses his arms over his chest. "Look, I get you don't really like me." He raises an eyebrow and continues, "Yeah, we kissed last year, and then it was pushed aside because *you* had a boyfriend. You're no better than him. I know I'm not everyone's cup of tea, but I think you need to take a real hard look in the mirror, Addison."

I stare at him, my mouth hanging open. I make a

coughing sound. "I'm *nothing* like Hayden Masters. I owned my mistake and told him what I did. I'm not perfect, Parker, I get it. But I'd never treat someone the way *he* treated me after the kiss we shared." I'm yelling and getting funny looks from pedestrians as they pass by. My throat tightens with emotion. Tears threaten. I shouldn't have to explain myself to him.

The only sound between Parker and me is the traffic. I need to leave, to run, to clear my head once again. *Why does this keep happening?*

"Don't assume to know me, Parker, because you don't. You actually know very little about me. See ya around." I run off as fast as my legs will carry me.

Tears slide down my cheeks, and are left in the wind. Yet again, another conversation with Parker down the drain. He assumes so much. I also think he might know me better than I know myself. We may not have spoken much since our kiss last year, but I've always felt his focus on me. Following me. Appraising me.

Why, I'm not sure.

CHAPTER
Seven

My phone alerts me to another message. I take it from my pocket.

"Urgh. Come on. Leave me alone." Rolling my eyes, I delete the message from Hayden. He's been non-stop with them lately.

"What a dick. Have you heard from Ella?" Elsie asks as we walk to our next class.

I stuff my phone back in my pocket. "No, not a word. We have a family dinner on Sunday, so it'll be interesting to see how that plays out. Any time I've seen her here she quickly busies herself in an attempt to avoid me." Not that I care too much for her at this point in time.

"What a cow. What kind of sister does something like that?"

I shrug. "Your guess is as good as mine."

"Look out, look out, there's a tramp about."

I look at Elsie, grinning at what she's said. She's giving death stares to someone, so I follow her line of sight, straight to Stacey standing in front of me. Her pouty red lips are plumped out, as though they've been injected with something to enhance them.

Stacey throws a hateful look to Elsie, who smiles pleasantly at her. "Shut it, bitch," Stacey says.

"Can I help you with something, Stacey?" I question curtly, not allowing her to get under my skin.

Stacey laughs, and my hands twitch. I want to block my ears or maybe even slap her.

"You think Parker would go for someone like you? You better stay away from him. He's mine!" Stacey says.

Now it's my turn to laugh in her face. Elsie joins in, and I compose myself after a moment. "Stacey, I don't know what drugs you've been smoking lately, but there's no way I'd go near Parker in that kind of way..." I pause, placing my index finger over my lips as though I'm pondering something. "Are you sure he even wants you back? If he does, he's stupid."

Stacey stamps her foot like a five-year-old throwing a tantrum. "Pfft. He'll come crawling back to me by the end of the week. He needs this. He *loves* it." She gestures to her body.

"Yeah, you keep telling yourself that if it makes you feel better," I say before stepping around her and her two other misfits with their plumped up lips and dishcloths for clothes.

"Suck it," Elsie hisses at Stacey as we stride away with our heads held high.

"Can you believe her?" I ask Elsie.

"I wonder why she's got that thought stuck in her head. You don't have anything to do with him, do you?"

She speaks the last two words very slowly. *Does she know something I don't?*

I shrug, shaking my head. "I don't have anything to do with him. After he beat Hayden up, he walked me back to campus. I dropped him on his ass with a karate move, and he's insulted me twice since then. So yeah, I'm fine not having anything to do with him. If he wants to go back to her, then I wish him all the luck in the world, because he'll need it." I purposely choose not to mention the way that Parker makes my chest squeeze tightly. Or how his touch ignites a swarm of sensations in my stomach. Those feelings are nothing but artificial, and they're only happening now because I'm vulnerable after what happened with Hayden and Stacey.

Elsie stops. I grin at her as her mouth hangs open in shock.

"What?" I hold my arms out, shrugging, unsure of her sudden demeanor.

"He walked you back, and you dropped him?" A devious smirk spreads across her features, and I already know what she's getting at.

"Nope. You clear that from your head right away." I slap her shoulder and keep walking to English.

"Oh, come on. Why not have a little fun at Stacey's expense, and also Hayden's? Oh, my hell, that would be brilliant…" She claps excitedly, clearly missing the furious shaking of my head.

"No, Elsie. Did you miss the part where I said he insulted me the last two times we've come face-to-face?"

"Oh, who cares about that? I want to see Hayden and Stacey's reactions." Her laughter continues on.

I shake my head furiously. "It's not going to happen. No more dating for me."

"Oh, come on, Addy. Don't be like that." She wraps her arm around my waist, pulling me closer to her. "Let's have a little fun. I'm going to find us the biggest, baddest parties to hit this weekend. So be prepared to go to work with a hangover on Saturday, and then we'll repeat it Saturday night."

Actually, it doesn't sound so bad to enjoy myself, since I haven't in a long time.

"Well, I'm down for the parties, but no Parker, and no other guys. Got that?" I give her a pointed stare, attempting to drive my point home.

Elsie pouts. "Whatever, you party pooper. Here's your class. I'll meet you here when you get out."

We say our goodbyes, and I step into my classroom. I release a sigh of relief, Parker's not here yet.

I take a seat in the second row, right in the middle. I don't want to get caught next to Parker again. We're like oil and water. Whenever we come into contact, we don't mesh well.

After about five minutes I hear high heels clicking into the room. My head flicks up and Mrs. Wilson marches in with a bowl, filled with what looks to be scrunched paper. Not two minutes later, Parker strides in and I'm entranced by his movements. He's damn good-looking in his fitted black tee and black basketball shorts. *Are they the only kinds of shorts he owns?* He looks up and scans the room.

Please don't sit next to me. I keep my head down, staring at the black screen of my cell phone. "Please don't. Please don't," I beg under my breath.

A body sits beside me. I don't move. I remain focused on my small wooden desk. My fingers trace the scratches previous students have made on the desk, as though I need to learn them for an assignment.

"Are those marks telling you a good story?"

I jump when I hear that sweet voice in my ear. I twist to my left. Parker rests back in his seat.

"At least they're much nicer to me than the company I have sitting beside me," I bite back.

A vast pearly white smile spreads across his face. He has a dimple on his right cheek I hadn't noticed before. "Oh, little mouse, I love your little nibbles." He chuckles.

I'm about to rebut when the teacher calling my name stops me.

"Addison! Could you please pay attention, as you're distracting the class with your chatter."

My face heats up. I'm sure it's turning the shade of my red tank top. *I think Mrs. Wilson has it in for me.* "Sorry, Mrs. Wilson."

She peers at me before continuing, "Now, as I was saying… we're going to do a paired book report. We'll be choosing our pairs out of this bowl. I've put half the class names in the bowl, and the other half will choose their partner. Addison, since you're so keen, how about you go first?"

Perfect. More embarrassment.

Standing, I step in front of Parker, my butt toward him. I'd prefer that than having to face him. I'm 100 percent sure he's checking out my ass as well.

I reach my hand in the bowl. I know I've got a very slim chance of picking Parker because there's probably about fourteen names in that jar. I have to hope he's a picker, and not a name. I shuffle the folded pieces of paper around and pull out one neatly folded piece.

With shaky hands, I slowly unfold it.

Parker Kent.

Of course.

The universe has it in for me.

"Read out who you've been partnered with, please," Mrs. Wilson says.

I really don't want to. Sucking in a deep breath, I say, "Parker Kent." My voice trembles as I read his name.

I watch his face light up, and I'm not sure why, but I have a sudden urge to drop him on his ass again.

"Thank you. Go and sit with your partner."

I walk back to my seat in a daze. *Why does stuff like this keep happening?* Sliding past Parker again, I feel the heat of a hand through my jeans on my thigh. Moving quickly, I fall back into my chair.

Leaning over toward Parker, annoyance fires through my veins. I whisper into his ear. "Do not touch me without my permission ever again," I seethe. Still, that mischievous grin doesn't shift off his face. That same dimple taunts me with its cuteness. Damn him.

"Come on now, partner. We're going to be stuck together for a while. You'll learn to love me."

Is he kidding himself? I'm not sure what kind of game he's playing at. I have no intention of getting involved either way.

"Maybe I'll see if someone can swap with me?" I already know that won't be allowed.

"Ouch, little mouse," he mocks, his hand gripping his chest dramatically.

Damn, he frustrates the living hell out of me, and it's clear he gets his kicks from me arguing with him. It's better for me to ignore him and stick to my guns.

The *lovely* Mrs. Wilson drones on about Shakespeare and something else. After half the lesson has gone by, I zone out, trying my hardest not to acknowledge the person beside me who keeps looking my way. His scent wraps around me, and slowly puts me under his spell. A spell I don't want to have any part of.

While taking some notes down, a neatly folded piece of paper is placed right on top of where I was writing. I push it out of my way and finish what I was doing.

Mrs. Wilson announces the end of class. I pack my books, and shove the note away in my jeans pocket.

"I'll be seeing you later, little mouse," Parker whispers in my ear.

My stomach clenches, and I pause. My breath hitches in my throat. Slowly, I turn toward him, but he's not there. He keeps doing stuff like this. Getting close, the letters, whispering seductively in my ear, it twists up my insides and makes them go crazy.

Rising from my chair, I walk out to find the last person I want to talk to in the hallway: Hayden. Elsie isn't here like she said she'd be. My eyes dart left and right, and something catches my attention. Parker stands at the end on my right, watching me. His stare isn't a playful one. He's ready to attack. The hate he holds for Hayden is more than evident in his dark glare.

Turning away from Hayden, I attempt an escape. For some reason, I go the way Parker is. When I look back to where he was standing, my heart sinks. He's gone. And here I was thinking he was going to be my back up if I needed him.

Hayden comes after me. "Addy, baby. Please talk to me," he begs.

That's something I've never heard from him. It's usually me doing the begging for him to not be angry at me.

"Go away, Hayden. I don't want to talk to you." I gain some speed. He grabs my arm, and I whip around, pulling it from his grasp. "Take the hint and leave me alone. We're done."

Hayden hangs his head, and when he looks up, I stop. Hayden has tears in his eyes. My chest tightens.

"Please, Addy. I miss you." An actual tear slides down his reddened face. I feel bad for him, and I know I shouldn't. He steps closer to me. I let him. I'm not sure why. He's never shown this kind of emotion before. "It's only fair you forgive me this time."

Did I hear that right? I move away from him.

"How dare you?" I hiss. "Yes, I made a mistake, and you've taken full advantage of that with the way you've treated me."

Hayden scoffs. The vulnerable side he showed seconds earlier is nowhere to be seen. *What a liar.*

"You think you're something so special. Let me tell you something: you're not. At least your sister was a better lay than you."

Everything in my vision shimmers red. My hands clench. My nails pierce the soft skin of my palm. I raise my fist and swing. It connects with Hayden's already colored cheek.

Hayden holds his face, staring at me like a deer stuck in headlights.

That felt amazing.

I should have done it sooner.

I hear laughter behind me. I spin on my heel. Parker and Elsie stand there, gripping their ribs as they laugh together. Tears fill her eyes.

"I should have let you take him on the other night," Parker says.

I feel damn proud of my punch. Thanks to karate and kickboxing, I didn't injure my hand. If Hayden had actually paid attention to the things I was doing, he would have had some idea to not confront me.

"You bitch," Hayden jeers.

I turn back to face him, not able to deal with this anymore. I step up to him, mustering all my courage. "Hayden… things between us are over. If you say my sister is better than me, maybe you should be dating her. I couldn't care less." I back away from him and walk toward Elsie and Parker, who both have huge-ass grins on their faces that match my own.

Parker throws his arm over my shoulder. I watch Elsie eye the exchange between him and me. I can see her brain is ticking over, and I'm sure I'll hear another of her Parker spiels when it's just us two alone together.

"Well, now, look at you go, little mouse." Parker chuckles.

"I told you the other night I could handle myself," I state, matter-of-factly.

"You should have believed her," Elsie jumps in.

"Next time, I'll leave you to your own defenses."

"Well, now you know. Come on, Elsie, let's get to our next classes. Catch ya around, Parker." My chest flutters being close to him. I quickly shrug out of his arm, not liking the way my body is reacting and betraying me.

I hook my arm with Elsie's and we take off, leaving Parker standing there openmouthed. I glance back, and he's still there… watching.

CHAPTER

Eight

Finally, the weekend arrives. I couldn't be happier to see the close of this long, drawn-out week.

Hayden, Stacey, and Ella—I've got nothing else to give in regards to these people. I plan to get wasted tonight. I'm overdue for some fun.

Arriving back at the dorm, before I've even opened the door I hear the music vibrating against the walls. Stepping inside, I'm greeted with my girls strutting around in their matching bras and lacy underwear as they swap and trade each other's clothes. The scent of beer and pizza strikes my nostrils, and my stomach grumbles as I realize I skipped lunch today. After my run-ins with Hayden, I didn't want to risk facing him again, so I went to the library instead for some quiet.

"Sweet cheeks is here," Willow announces to the entire building.

All the girls cheer.

Willow comes toward me. I can tell she's already had a fair few drinks, and it's only six p.m. Tonight's going to be crazy.

Willow opens her arms and hugs me, and I give her one back. "Are you ready to party? We're heading to a frat house for some fun tonight. You said no Hayden or Parker, so we're going somewhere they'll most likely not be." She kisses my cheek and releases me, going back to her room. *I better not get too drunk tonight, especially if Willow's already in that state.*

Elsie struts up to me in a fitted short black spaghetti strap dress. It has roses embellished over the fabric. It's a beautiful dress which sits just above her knees. "Come on, girl, let's get you a beer and some food. We've got to get you all dolled up for a night of fun and laughter with the girls, and… maybe some guys."

I give her the evil eye. "I'm happy with no guys. I just want to be with you girls."

Elsie strips me of my backpack and thrusts a chilled beer in one hand and a plate with a slice of pizza in the other. I take a bite as she leads me to our room, shutting the door behind her. She doesn't say anything. She goes to her cupboard and begins digging through it, and after a moment, she produces a shopping bag.

"I bought this for you. No returns, and you have to wear it tonight. If you don't, it'll break my heart. It can be a breakup gift." From the bag, she pulls out a navy blue dress. It looks similar to hers, but there are no roses on it.

"Elsie, can't I wear a pair of jeans? I'm not a dress kinda girl, and you know that."

She shakes her head. "I swear you've been in those same jeans for the last three days."

She could be right. If I can get away with not washing them every day, I'll do it.

I place the food and drink down. Wiping the grease from my fingertips, I take the dress from her. It hangs off its spaghetti straps on both my index fingers.

I'm unsure. It's a beautiful dress, only it's not me.

"Addy, listen to me. You need to start stepping out of the little box Hayden shoved you in. Be that outrageous girl I first met when we arrived in a shared dorm together last year."

Deep within me, I know she's right. I need to step out again. Get the confidence back and be the girl who doesn't care.

"We'll see. Now, get out, and let me get dressed."

Elsie jumps up and down excitedly, cheering as she leaves the room.

I stare at the dress. *Guess I'd better get to it.* I empty my jeans pockets before taking them off. My fingertip grazes something. Pulling it out, I realize it's the note from Parker. Slowly, I open it. Again, there's a number on it. *What's he playing at?*

Taking my cell from my back pocket, I put the number into my phone under Parker's name. I decide to play a little game of *Guess Who*.

Addison: Who is this?

Hitting send, a grin spreads across my face.

I tear off my clothes and pull the silky material over my body. It glides on perfectly, and sits nicely in the places it should. I run my hands down the front while looking down at myself. From this angle, it looks great, but I'm still unsure. I go and stand in front of our full-length mirror.

My mouth drops at the sight before me. I actually look beautiful. The dress sits above my knees, like Elsie's. Of course the dress hugs her body more. It suits her, but it suits my body style too. It has a V-neck which comes low and exposes some cleavage. The other difference to Elsie's is mine has a lower back, with straps that crisscross down to about the middle of my back. I feel sexy, and ready to step out and have some fun.

"Look at you," Elsie exclaims from the doorway.

I jump, not expecting her to be there. "You gave me a heart attack, Elsie."

She comes and stands beside me, assessing my outfit. "I knew it would be a flawless fit on you. I have a talent for picking the perfect outfit. Now, let's do your makeup and hair."

"What's wrong with how I look now? I don't want to look too out there. I love the dress, and maybe it's enough for now." The extent of my makeup is usually foundation, eyeliner, and some light pink lip gloss when I go out. I don't even wear makeup during the day.

Elsie takes my hand, dragging me out of our room and to a chair which sits beside our little secondhand dining table. The table is covered in a heap of different shades of eye shadows, blushes, lipsticks, and things I don't recognize. Elsie forces my butt onto the waiting seat, races off, and comes back with my food and drink.

"Now, make sure you eat. I don't need you to be an easy drunk tonight. I'll start with your eyes. Shut them."

I do as she says. "Gee, bossy much? Is this what you're like in the bedroom?" I giggle.

"You'll never know."

Shoving a large piece of pizza in my mouth, I take a bite of its cheesy goodness. *I wonder if Parker has messaged me back.*

Elsie gets busy applying some foundation and blush, then begins on my eyes.

"Don't go too crazy, girl," I warn her.

"Oh, let loose tonight, Addy. Who cares what people think? Just have fun."

Easy for her to say. I haven't been to a proper party for twelve months.

"I'll try." And I will. I need to rediscover who I am and find my happy medium again. I've been stuck in this unhappy rut for far too long.

The little brushes tickle my eyelids, and I already know I'm going to look the complete opposite of what I did thirty minutes ago.

"Have you heard from Parker?" she whispers, so none of the other girls overhear. They were still marching around in their underwear when Elsie brought me out here. I love that we can be so comfortable with each other. These girls are more like sisters than my own flesh and blood.

"No."

"Really? Nothing?" she questions, as if I should have heard something.

"Nothing. Remember, guy-free for a while, I think."

She scoffs at my words. "Come on, Addison. Don't do this to me."

"Do what?"

"Block out the male species because your ex-boyfriend was a dickhead."

"I need a break for a little bit." I sigh. She doesn't understand. She's never been serious with anyone who I've noticed, or who she's told me about. I know Elsie likes to keep her options open, and if something tickles her fancy, she'll grab the opportunity with both hands.

"Have you heard from your bitch of a sister?"

I don't want to hear from her. "No, and that's fine with me. I'll most likely see her at family dinner on Sunday. Might need a few drinks before I go face her."

Elsie grips my bare shoulders. "I've got your back."

Those four words hold promise. She'll always have my back. I couldn't get through all of this without Elsie.

She applies the final touches to my lips. "Open your eyes."

I nervously do what she says. When I do, Elsie is holding a mirror in front of me and I come face-to-face with a new Addison I've never met before.

"Wow," I breathe. The look she's given me is smoky with gold on the inner part of my eyes, and bright red lips which say, 'kiss me.' I've never had this much makeup on my face. Ever. "Wow," I repeat.

"Girls, come look at our supermodel, Addison."

Screams greet me when they see me.

"You look stunning, Addy," Jane says excitedly, with a hint of awe. "Elsie, please do me next."

I stand, giving her the seat. She sits, closing her eyes, and awaits her turn.

"Wowsers! Addy will be picking up tonight," cries Willow. She makes me do a twirl, then races off, yelling, "I have the perfect shoes for you!"

She comes back with a pair of shimmery gold strappy heels.

"They're great. They'll kill my feet though. They look like they're five inches high."

Willow gives me a *whatever* eye roll.

I'm most likely exaggerating about the height.

"Addy, put them on." She thrusts them at me, and I go sit on the couch and slip the first one on my foot. It fits perfectly. The shoe's got a pointy toe with straps which tie up around the ankle, like how the Ancient Romans tied their sandals. Now, if these were flat, they would appeal to me so much more. Comfort all the way. As I tie them up, the straps come halfway up my leg. Once I finish, I make my way back to the full-length mirror in my room.

I'm blown away. It's not me; it's a new Addison.

I like her. I feel more confident already in this outfit and the makeup. Elsie is so good with this stuff. A small part of me wants to run into either Ella or Hayden just to smear it in their faces, to show them they can't bring me down. I'm stronger than either of them realize.

I pick a clutch purse out of the collection Elsie has stored in her cupboard. I collect my cell from my bedside table, and when I pick it up, there's a message. Tingles flitter within me when I see it's from Parker.

Parker: I should be asking who this is.

I grin stupidly at my phone. What can I say back? My fingers hover.

Addison: That's for me to know and for you to find out.

CHAPTER Nine

We finally arrive at the frat house around eleven p.m. after tossing down some shots of tequila. I'm feeling pretty loose and ready to have fun tonight. I want to dance and enjoy being free.

We walk in like we own the place. All heads turn to us for a moment, then people go back to their conversations.

It's a large house; the furniture's been pushed back against the walls. A DJ is set up in one corner of the living room, and the bass is vibrating through every inch of me. I scan the room, taking in who's here, and who I know.

"Wow! This place is packed," Elsie yells into my ear over the music. "Wanna get a drink?"

I nod, and we all head toward the kitchen.

"Looking good, Addy."

I turn at the mention of my name. Jase stands there,

his blond hair slicked nicely, and his navy shirt clinging to his bulging body. Muscles on muscles.

"Hey, Jase! How are you?" I'm super thankful I've had those drinks now.

Elsie grabs my elbow, and says, "I'll go get us a drink and come find you."

I smile, nodding as Jase steps closer.

"He's not here, just so you know," Jase says.

I know who he's referring to. I move closer to Jase, and he puts his arm around my shoulder, pulling me into his side. It feels nice. He guides me out the back door, and onto the large green lawn where scattered groups are all standing around, chatting amongst each other.

Mouths fall open at the sight of me. I'm even gifted with some wolf whistles, which makes my heart sing. I'm not sure who from. Damn, I feel like I'm floating on cloud nine. Finally, I'm part of the crowd. I'm no longer Hayden Masters's girlfriend. I'm the new and improved Addison James.

"Jase, he's not going to get to me tonight. I'm so done with his drama." The bitterness toward Hayden rolls off my tongue.

"I love this look on you, Addy." His warm hand rubs my upper arm. I immediately want to pull my arm away. Jase has never been like this with me. I don't look at him like someone I'd date.

I smile up at him. "Thanks. It's very new." I laugh.

Jase guides me to some empty seats, we sit and fall into a comfortable silence.

"Jase, I just want to say thanks for looking out for me the other night."

He takes my hand and says, "Addy, I'd do it again. I

wish I would have done something sooner." His fingers tighten around my own, gently I pull my hand out of his and pretend to swipe away a hair in my face.

"I bet you were in some serious trouble with your team, especially Hayden."

Jase relaxes back in his chair, releasing my hand. "I don't care about him. He's a dick who doesn't deserve you. You're too good for him."

I wonder where all the niceties are coming from. I've spoken to Jase a number of times before, only he's never ever talked to me the way he is now. And all the touchy-feely moves from him make me want to go find Elsie. I only see him as a friend.

At that moment, Elsie waltzes through the back door. She spots us easily enough, makes her way over, and takes a spot on another empty seat. She hands me a cup of beer along with another shot. I eye her skeptically.

"What? It's what you had earlier, back at the dorm." She giggles before throwing down her own shot. I follow suit, a low hiss comes from me as the burn follows through.

"Hi, I'm Elsie." Elsie extends her hand toward Jase, who takes it.

"I'm Jase."

"Nice to meet you. I've seen you around, but never actually spoken to you," Elsie says with such confidence. That's her—she doesn't need alcohol to get her chatting, but add alcohol and you get mega chatty Elsie.

"Yeah, you, too," Jase says before his gaze darts behind me.

His demeanor immediately changes. He bolts upright as though he's been shocked by an electric current.

I turn to see what's caused this change. Of course, only two people could do that.

Hayden and Ella have graced us with their presence. *Perfect!*

Jase curses under his breath, as does Elsie. She's out of her chair as fast as Jase and by my side. She grips my arm, pulling me to my feet. Slowly, I manage to get to my feet. This is a massive blow. Of course, I told Hayden to date my sister. I just never really expected him to do so.

"Wait right here," Jase says, his tone hard and unreadable. He stalks toward Ella and Hayden. He greets them happily enough, shaking hands and giving them a one-armed hug.

"Let's leave. We can find another party to go to." Elsie attempts to pull me along.

I'm rooted to the spot. I stare at the gracious pair of cheaters as they walk around the yard as if they're the king and queen. Ella laughs at something Hayden says, while I swallow the lump that's formed in my throat.

This shouldn't get to me. Neither of them deserve my tears.

I storm off inside to retrieve another drink. After grabbing an unopened bottle of tequila, I crack the lid. Finding two clean, empty shot glasses, I turn toward Elsie. "Are you all in?"

An evil smirk slides across her beautiful face, and I know she's with me. "Of course."

"Count us in as well." Willow and Jane come from nowhere and hold out their glasses.

I pour us all one. "To freedom." I salute my glass up high, and they follow. "To freedom."

"And tequila," Elsie says.

We all burst out laughing, then down our shots. I refill the glasses.

About fifteen or maybe twenty minutes later, Jase struts into the kitchen eyeing all of us. His gaze is wild, angry even. I'm so wasted. I pick up the bottle ready to pour another, and realize it's got enough for one more round. May as well finish off the contents.

"Don't you think you've had enough, girls?" Jase asks as he takes the empty bottle from my grasp. I couldn't care less about what he thinks. He abandoned me the moment Hayden and Miss Slut waltzed in.

"What do you care?" I slur, followed by more laughter. "Let's go dance, girls!" I shout, and they cheer.

"Addy, don't do this. You're allowing him to get the better of you."

"You do realize that's my sister he came with. I don't care how I appear to anyone, especially him or her. They deserve each other. And as for me, I'm better off with no one. Guys are dickheads."

I'm yanked away from him and shoved on the dance floor by Elsie. We dance and roll our bodies against each other, trying out new moves. We don't care how silly we look. It's all about the fun.

"I gotta go pee," I shout in Elsie's ear.

"I'm coming."

We tell the other two, and make our way off the dance floor through the living room. Sweat trickles down my back. I've never felt as limitless as I do right in this moment. If I'm sweaty and gross, at least it'll keep guys at bay. Jase hasn't come near me again.

"Have you seen *them* again?" Elsie asks as we walk to the bathroom.

I shake my head and pull my cell from the clutch I have dangling off my shoulder. I haven't checked it since arriving at the party, and it's now one thirty a.m. I have three messages from Parker. *He deserves an earful as well.*

I hit his name and put the phone to my ear while Elsie gives me a puzzled look. "Who are you calling this late?"

"Parker Kent."

Elsie dives at me. "No, hang up!" she screeches, and attempts to rip the phone away from my grasp. I twist in the opposite direction to her attacks. I may be drunk, although I'm not wholly and incoherently wasted. I know exactly what I'm doing. At least, I think I do.

"Get lost." I bat her hand away once again.

Parker answers on the fourth ring. "Hello…"

I stop, then Elsie stops, and her eyes are wide.

His voice is like sweet honey. "Who is this?"

I need to respond. *Answer, you loser.*

Elsie waves her hands in front of my face. "Did he answer?" she whispers.

I clear my parched throat and finally respond, "Parker," I breathe.

"Addison? Is that you?" I hear the cockiness behind his questions, and it grates on my very last nerve.

"Of course it is. You gave me your number *twice*. Did you think I'd never use it?" I say, finding my voice.

I hear his laughter and sounds from people around him. *Is he out at another party?*

A girl's giggle comes through the phone, and I cringe. "I'll leave you be." I don't allow him to respond and hang up.

What the ever-loving hell was I thinking? I need another drink.

"What happened?" Elsie pounces on me like a tiger on its prey.

"Nothing. He was busy," I state. I'm unable to shake the unnerving feeling brewing deep in my stomach. I'm not sure if it's a good or bad feeling. I can't even explain it to my brain in this moment. "I need another drink. Now!"

When we finish our business, I go to the kitchen to grab another beer. Elsie's in shock about the phone call and continues to tell me how stupid I am.

Not looking where I'm going, I stride straight into a hard body.

"Oh, sorry," I say, then look up, and I'm suddenly face-to-face with Hayden. He smiles, and it's not a charming one. It's a slimeball one. "Oh, it's you. I retract my apology. I hope it hurt." Even though I know it wouldn't have, I can hope.

"Adddiiisssooonnn," he slurs.

And here I thought I was drunk. Apparently, not as bad as him.

I wrinkle my nose up and step around him to the fridge. Elsie flanks me.

"You look sexy, Addy. We could have a quickie, for old time's sake."

I almost choke on the first mouthful of my drink. Wiping the dribbles away that escape when choking, I respond, "Yeah, of course. I'll just go tell my sister, and maybe she can give me a few pointers on how to please you since apparently, I didn't do it right the first time."

Hayden slides onto the bench, gazing at me. "You want to know what your problem is, Addy?"

"Please enlighten me." I casually lean against the fridge, as does Elsie.

"You were boring. Plain and simple. Just boring. I need some excitement."

I cock an eyebrow. "Hmm... okay... maybe I'll work on that for the next guy I get with."

I'm suddenly feeling too sober for this conversation. I go to where the drinks are located and make myself the strongest concoction and add some ice. I'm not sure what exactly I pour into the glass, yet every mouthful I take burns my throat. It's glorious.

Turning around, I see Hayden's still there. Hate stares back at me. He's angry about something.

"Something wrong?" I gift him a threatening smile.

"Are you dating Parker Kent?"

"What?" I choke.

"Are. You. Dating. Parker. Kent?" he repeats it very slowly, as though I'm stupid or something.

"Yeah, I think you're messed in the head. Really, though, it's none of your concern who I see." I take another gulp of the chilled drink, and I can already feel my head starting to swim with fogginess. "This conversation is over. Tell Ella I said hey. I hope you're happy." I raise my glass to him. "Here's to you and your pathetic life." I chug the remaining half of my glass, placing the empty cup on the counter. Yeah, that in itself was a terrible idea. I cough thanks to the burning sensation which has now settled in my chest.

I reach out and grip Elsie's wrist. "Let's go."

She puts a caring arm around my shoulders and leads me out the back door, right into the back of the yard where no one's around.

"Sit," she says.

I collapse in a mess on the neatly trimmed green grass. "I hate my life, Elsie."

"Oh, come on now. Don't let him affect you like that. Where's the sassy, sexy bitch who came here with me?" She comes down beside me, throwing her arms around me and squeezing me tight before releasing her hold. We rest against the white picket fence, staring back at the house which is still buzzing with excitement. I spot my sister and Hayden slipping around the side of the house holding hands. Ella snickers like a silly girl.

I don't want it to affect me, however, it does.

"Why do I have a sister who's such a bitch... slut... whatever you want to call her? Who does what she did to their own blood?" Tears brim in my eyes. I quickly rub them away so they don't have the chance to fall.

"Oh, honey, don't punish yourself with those kinds of thoughts. You know exactly the type of person your sister and ex-boyfriend are."

"Perhaps he's right... I'm a boring person."

"Don't you dare say that!" Anger flares in her tone. "Never let him make you feel like crap again. You're so much better than those two put together." She throws her hands toward the house.

We fall silent. It's peaceful. "I don't remember right now if I told you, but last year toward the end of the year, I came to a party and ended up kissing Parker Kent."

Elsie chuckles beside me. "Girl, you must be wasted because that made its way around school like the video of Parker laying those punches on Hayden the other night. It spread like wildfire. Everyone thought you were lucky Hayden didn't leave you."

I wish he had. "Look where it got me though. He was so terrible to me after that night. I told him right after it happened, and since then he became controlling."

"Yeah, I could tell. I'm sorry. As your friend, I should have done more."

I turn to look at her. Her head hangs low, and her face is surrounded by her long locks. "Elsie, you were there for me when I needed you. I'm not mad at you. It was always up to me to leave him, and I guess it took me a damn long time." I laugh, and she gives me a semi-smile. "It was all on me, not you."

Lifting her head, she stares at the house again. "Love ya. Even if you are an airy-fairy." Using her nickname I've given her. I shove her shoulder playfully.

"Love you. Even if you're stupidly drunk right now. I love the laidback sweet cheeks."

We throw our heads back, cackling.

"What's so hilarious, and why aren't I invited to the party?"

We stop abruptly, and I focus on the figure before me, silhouetted thanks to the bright lights shining behind him.

But I'd know that voice anywhere.

Parker.

"What the heck? How did you find me?"

"Oh, little mouse…" Parker chuckles, and my body ignites at the sound.

I hate you body. You betray me all the damn time.

CHAPTER Ten

I stare up at this godly figure. I don't need to see his face to know he's wearing one of his flirtatious grins—the one all the girls seem to fall over each other for.

"When will you learn I know all?" He smiles. "By the way, you look sexy tonight, little mouse."

My cheeks heat at Parker's compliment.

"I have these for you." He steps closer, handing Elsie and I a fresh cold beer each.

Elsie eagerly takes hers, throwing back a mouthful.

I'm a little hesitant. I'm still fuzzy in the head from the crazy cocktail I mixed earlier. "Why are you here?" I ask, rubbing my finger around the top of the bottle, then lifting it and taking a mouthful. *Cool and refreshing.*

"You rang, and I came. Figured you had something you wanted to say to me." Parker goes and grabs himself a seat on the grass beside me. He places his beer to his lips. His lips... wow. I'd love to bring mine to them, suck on them, kiss them, bite them...

I lean against the fence, Elsie pipes up, "She's pretty wasted, and was going to mouth off at you."

My head whips toward her, my mouth hanging open. "Elsie," I cry. *Gosh, she's a little chatterbox when she's had some drinks.*

Parker gives one of his full-belly rumble laughs. "No, Elsie, please keep going." He leans forward, waiting. There's a good distance between us, yet I can still make out his woodsy scent. It does crazy things to me.

"Well, I, personally, think you guys should date to get back at those two cheaters." She throws the word 'cheaters' out like it's a foul piece of food.

I turn and frown at Elsie. She smiles.

"What are you doing?" I hiss in a low tone. I know Parker can still hear me, but I don't care.

"Not a bad idea. What do you say, little mouse?" Parker asks.

"No. I'm out of the dating game."

Parker raises his eyebrows in question. "No dating, huh? Well, that's not going to work, is it?"

"No, it's not going to work. I'm especially not going to date guys like you, who have girls falling all over themselves in the hope you'll talk to or even acknowledge them."

"I can't help the fact I'm loved so much." Parker sighs, sitting upright.

"Yeah, not by everyone," I reply dryly.

Elsie, breaks out in laughter. Parker and I turn toward her. "What's so funny, Elsie?" I ask.

"Oh, you two. Don't you see the chemistry between you both?"

"Yeah, I think you've had too much to drink, and right now I need another one. A super-strong one again."

"You already have one." Parker gestures to the bottle I'm clutching in my hand.

"Well I better finish it then." Lifting it to my lips, I scull down the remainder of my beer before tossing the bottle to the grass. Standing, I go toward the house, not caring that I'm leaving Elsie and Parker there. *Heck, she can date him for all I care.*

Back in the kitchen, the music in the living room a dull thud in here, and thankfully, there doesn't seem to be anyone around. I need some space. I pour another cocktail of drinks into another cup, like I did before. This time, it's a much larger red cup. *Bring it on.*

Loud, chatty voices float through the back door, and my blood runs cold. *Ella.* I stop what I'm doing and listen.

"Come on, baby. Let's take this home," Ella's high-pitched whiney voice says.

"Not yet," Hayden gruffs out. *He doesn't sound happy about something.*

"Who cares about him? Let him have her if he wants her."

Who are they talking about? I remain still with the bottle of alcohol in my hand. I know I shouldn't be listening, except I can't help myself.

"I don't care about them," he growls. There's that tone I know all too well. Ella must be deaf not to hear that bitterness in his voice.

"Whatever. You're only here with me because you knew *she* would be here. You're just using me to get to her." There's silence followed by footsteps coming inside. I quickly get back to mixing my concoction, because I'm sure I'll need it in a moment or two. I sense eyes staring at my back.

"Well, well, well..." Ella's voice is cold and unwelcoming.

I don't respond. Instead, I finish what I'm doing, then slowly turn around. She stands there in her short red strapless dress that shows her butt.

"Oh, hey there, you two. Don't you both look so adorable together?" I squeak out with as much cuteness as I can, even though the words leave a sour taste in my mouth. I wash it away with a mouthful of my drink, and it's like acid's being poured down my throat. *Perfect.* This is the mix I should have made myself earlier.

Ella gives me the evil eye. *What did I ever do to her for her to hate me so much?*

"Don't play the sweet game. You can't have him back," she throws the words out at me.

I take another few gulps and feel the courage within me grow stronger. "Why does everyone assume I want their boyfriends?" I raise my voice. A small group of people standing in the doorway turn toward us. Clearing my throat, I continue, "Now, slutty sister, I wouldn't want him. I wouldn't want him back after you'd had him. Who would want your sloppy seconds? Not me."

Ella's hands fly to her open mouth while Hayden's muscles flex. He shows no emotion what-so-ever. I never miss that twitch; it's his tic. I know he's angry, and what's more, I love my liquid courage.

Ella readjusts herself, raising her chin. As if I didn't just throw some hurtful words at her. She deserves them. "How dare you speak to me like that? You do realize I could make your life here one where you'd be miserable," she threatens.

Hayden does nothing, only stands there studying me. His eyes follow the length of my body. Ella could well make my life living hell, but I'm not going to let her get to me. I'll survive whatever she throws my way.

I throw back the rest of my drink, placing the cup on the bench. I'm done with this conversation. "Ella…" I let her name linger in the air for a moment. She crosses her arms over her chest, tapping her silver high heel and, releases a heavy sigh.

"Well?" she pushes.

I walk toward her, a cold look on my face. I smile, yet there's nothing pleasant about it. I stop short of her and Hayden. "Do your worst. I've lived with you my entire life. I know exactly what you're like. You can try and bring me down any way you want, but know this…" I glance at Hayden, then back to Ella. "He only came here tonight because I was here. I know it, and so do you. Are you happy being with someone who appears to not even like you? Good luck to you both."

I step around them and head out the back door toward Elsie and Parker, who are on their way toward me. Parker has a hard glare on his face.

"Hey, you two," I say.

"Are you all right?" Elsie asks, concern etched on her face. She wraps me in her arms.

Stepping back, I sway slightly. Parker catches my arm. It's a searing touch, and I don't pull away. Instead, I move closer, pressing the back of my body against his front. "Why wouldn't I be?"

Elsie looks at me, looks to Parker, and then to the door I walked out of. "Ah… did you talk to your sister?"

"Yep." I add a pop to the P.

"Did you get another drink?"

"Yep," I respond, popping the P again.

"Yep, and I drank the whole thing while talking to them."

Elsie's mouth falls open. "Was it as strong as the first one?"

I give her an evil grin. "Even worse because it burned the whole way down." I burp, and I can taste it all over again. Shit, that burns.

"Wow! You're seriously trashed, little mouse," Parker says.

He's right. "Why, yes, I am, hot shot." I snort with laughter. "Get it? Basketball. Hot shot. Gee, I hope you're a good shot." I snort again.

Elsie stares at me, tilting her head to the side. "I think you've lost it." She giggles.

I press farther back into Parker. His hand comes to my hip. Tingles shoot throughout my entire body. "Who cares? I'm done considering what others think. My sister threatened to ruin my life here." I cackle. "She really doesn't know me very well."

"I'd like to see her try," Parker grumbles under his breath. I'm not even sure if he really says it or not. I twist and look up at him, only his expression is unreadable.

"Perhaps it's time to go home. I'm sure you'll be feeling sore and sorry for yourself tomorrow, and you have to work early," Elsie says.

"Pfft… Jen will understand. I want to dance more. Where's Willow and Jane? They'll party with me." I step out of Parker's grasp, making my way into the house. I stumble with each step I take. *These shoes are going to be the death of me.*

"Willow... Jane... where are you?" The music's still pumping, and there are still heaps of people around. I hear two familiar screams coming from the dance floor. I make my way toward the sound, and my friends greet me with warm hugs. Elsie comes in behind me, then the girls stop dancing, and their focus falls on something behind me.

"What's up, ladies?" Parker asks. I hear the charm dripping from his words. He's such a womanizer.

I turn around, and he's inches from me. His hands find their places on my hips, and I want to melt into him, for him to wrap me up in those delicious arms. "Don't you have friends here? Where are your little followers?"

He chuckles, then leans into me. "They're here. But I figure I need to keep an eye on you because you're trashed." His breath tickles my bare shoulder. Goose bumps rise on my skin. "You smell so good. Simply mouthwatering." His warm hands wrap around my waist, pulling me flush against him.

"Parker, baby? Is that you?"

I hear his growl before he releases me, turning his back to me. Peeking around him, I see Stacey standing there in a skin-tight black leather strapless dress. Looks more like slut outfit to me. I'm yanked back into the folds of my friends.

Standing face-to-face, Stacey and Parker face off.

"Why are you with *her?*" Stacey jabs her finger at me.

I offer a smile her way, she tips her head to the side, before turning her attention back to Parker.

"I'm allowed to be. It's none of your concern anymore. I believe your fellow cheater is here as well." Parker shrugs.

The music stops. I spin around. A policeman stands in the doorway.

"Time to go," Elsie says, taking my hand and dragging me out the back door.

I want to stay and see what happens with Parker and Stacey. "Do we have to?"

"No, underage drinking here. Hello… is the switch on in here Addison?" She taps a finger on my head.

"Nope, she's left the building." I laugh.

"Come on." Elsie continues to pull me along, grunting and groaning. Willow and Jane have taken off and bailed on us. There's a swarm of people rushing to leave as well.

Suddenly, I'm taken hold of and spun around, then hoisted over someone's shoulder.

"What are you doing?" I scream. "Put me down!"

"Shut it, little mouse."

Parker.

"Do you mind? You're flashing my underwear to the world."

He laughs. "And yet, I'm not given the privilege."

I want to die. This is so embarrassing. "Elsie, get him to put me down." I'm really close to his ass. His nice ass.

"Nope. You're slowing me down, and we need to get out of here quick smart, thanks to whoever called the police."

"If I promise to walk faster will you put me down?"

"Sure," Parker says, stopping and placing me on my very tender feet.

Adjusting my clothes, I say, "Thanks."

Elsie claps her hands. "Come on, you two. Where are your buddies, Parker?"

Parker takes my hand in his and pulls me along, and I keep up as best I can. That last drink wasn't the best idea. "They took off. They can take care of themselves."

Once we're far enough away from the party, we fall into a slower pace, which is heaven sent. My feet are throbbing. "I need to take my shoes off," I say to Elsie, so I stop and steady myself, gripping Parker's arm. It tenses under my grip. My heels fall to the ground, and the arches of my feet seem to breathe a sigh of relief. "Oh, that feels so much better."

I collect my shoes off the ground, and Parker pulls me into his side. It feels nice and sets my body off.

No, Addison, don't go there.

There she is, the sensible me. Drinks are definitely wearing off.

Pulling away from him, I say, "We're good from here. Thanks for your help tonight, Parker."

We're only about five minutes from campus, which means his place isn't far away either. Turning the corner, I see the lights on at the house he lives in.

He doesn't let go of my hand even though I've pulled away from his side. "Looks like the boys have brought the party home. Wanna come hang there?" His eyes set on me, and drunk Addison wants to respond and continue with this—whatever it is that's going on between Parker and me.

Elsie cuts in before I can answer. "No, thanks. She has to work tomorrow, and I think I'm going to be holding her hair back for her at some stage this evening, or should I say morning. She doesn't usually drink this much."

"Oh, shhh, Elsie, you're ruining my fun."

Parker releases my hand. I want to reach for him but

refrain. He leans in close. "Was good seeing you tonight, little mouse." His lips brush the side of mine, and my breath leaves my lungs. He stands up, and I'm left gasping. "I'll see you girls later."

"Catch ya, Parker."

"Bye," I whisper, unable to raise my voice much higher.

Turning on his heel, he's gone.

Elsie whips around in front of me. "Oh. My. Goodness. Parker Kent almost kissed you," she squeals.

It's like a bucket of ice-cold water is poured over me.

He nearly did.

And I wanted him to.

I can't do this.

He's another player.

Put the guard back up, Addison.

CHAPTER Eleven

"Oh, hell. I feel like death," I mumble into my pillow.

Elsie grunts in response.

"What happened at the end of last night?" Things are a bit hazy. My brain is slowly showing me a slideshow of images, and some of them include me throwing my guts up, and only just making it to the bathroom.

"You puked everywhere," she mutters, before raising her head. "Are you going to work today?"

I want to throw myself out the window for allowing myself to get so trashed. "I guess so."

I reach for my cell. My hand finally connects with it after a few taps around on the cupboard beside my bed. I bring it closer and light it up. The clock reads seven a.m. I don't start until nine, which is a bonus.

"Elsie, I don't remember much about last night after

seeing Hayden in the kitchen. I remember running into him again, then not much after that." I shuffle onto my back. My stomach sways, and a wave of nausea rushes over me. I suck in some hard breaths, and eventually, it subsides.

She grunts rolling over. She has dark circles under her eyes from last night's makeup. If Elsie looks like that, I can only imagine what I must look like.

"Do you remember telling Hayden and Ella off?"

"I recall them being at the party and talking to Jase. Dancing. Chatting with you, and then Parker showed up, and from there, things become a little fuzzy."

"Oh, so you don't remember Parker pretty much kissing you, and you getting all cozy with him." She giggles, settling herself on to her side and facing me.

My hands cover my face. "No. Please tell me that didn't happen."

"Oh, it happened all right."

"I'm so stupid. Did I say anything I'll regret?"

Elsie goes silent for a moment. "Umm... no, I don't think so. You both got pretty touchy-feely with each other, and flirty."

I want to die. This is so bad.

"Why would you let me do that, Elsie? You're supposed to keep me away from people, especially guys like him." I'm not happy about hearing this information at all.

It's clear by the way Elsie sits up and frowns that she's not impressed with how I'm acting.

"Don't get all crabby at me. You were the one that downed those ridiculous drinks, not me. I looked out for you, and it appears Parker did as well. He came with us instead of going with his friends when the police showed up at the party."

"What? Police?"

She nods.

"I'm sorry, and count me out of any parties tonight. If I manage to make it through work it'll be a miracle. I feel so sick, if I move I think I might throw up." I wrap my arms over my unsettled stomach.

Elsie gives me a sad look, her bottom lip pouting. "Oh, honey, it's not like it's the first time you've been sick. You already brought up a hell of a lot last night." She laughs.

Work is going to be hell.

I sit at my parents' dinner table, shifting food around my plate. I wanted to leave the minute I walked through the door, especially when Ella arrived. I've been biting my tongue, literally, so not to cause a hassle. Mom carries on as if there's no tension sitting like an extra person at our dinner table.

"Mom, did you know Addison was drunk at a party on Friday night?" Ella says. My mouth falls open. I should have known that Ella would start something.

Siting up straighter, I look from Ella to Mom and say. "Mom, did she tell you that she slept with my now ex-boyfriend, Hayden? So don't start on me until you've heard the full story." I fold my arms across my chest, watching Mom and Dad's reaction. Dad stops eating midway through a forkful.

"Why are you girls always doing this? Always at each other's throats." Dad drops his cutlery onto his plate with a loud clang, before standing, his chair scraping along the wooden floor. "You two need to sort this out, or there will be consequences," he threatens.

I point to Ella. "She's the one with the problem." Devon stands and walks out of the room covering his ears. He doesn't cope well with conflict.

"Now look what you've done," Mom says gesturing to the empty doorway Devon had just left through.

"He'll be alright. I'll talk to him before I go. Also, did you speak to the school about the kids picking on Devon?" I ask.

She sighed. "Addison, please remember I'm the parent here."

I sighed and thought, *Sometimes I really wonder.*

"I've spoken to the principal, and she assured me things are being taken care of," Mom said.

I'd relaxed only a little with those words.

I stand. "I'm going. I've got lots of homework to do. I'll see you later Mom." I go place a kiss on her cheek before turning to Ella, who's still sitting. I scowl and walk away.

I find dad sitting in the study reading. I say goodbye and go in search of Devon. He's in his room with headphones on. I tap him on the shoulder, he turns and pauses his music.

"Sorry about dinner," I say gently rubbing his arm.

"Is it true what you said about Ella?" He fiddles with the hem of his shirt, not making eye contact with me.

"Yes, it's true," I reply.

"Can you two sort it out?" he asks, I sigh. "Devon, she's difficult. I don't know what I ever did to her for her to hate me so much."

"I know she can be difficult," Devon mumbles. I wrap my arm around his shoulders.

"Hey, Devon, I have to go. I'll talk to you later."

"Okay, Addy. Take care."

"You, too." I stand and leave. I need to get away from my sister.

I stare out the café window. The weekend was a blur. I managed to survive dinner. They're always tension filled.

I aimlessly wipe down the bench in front of me and tidy up a few tables that customers have left. Jen is out back doing bookwork and rosters.

Standing upright, I catch sight of Parker through the window. His arm is slung over one of the cheerleader's shoulders. I'm not sure of her name, so I'll call her *Barbie*. I chuckle inside. Her blonde high-top ponytail sits ridiculously high on her head, and when they walk through the door, her laugh is so damn fake. Could she be any more desperate?

I watch Parker and *Barbie* take a seat at a table in the corner. Hushed voices and giggles are all I hear, and a twinge of jealousy whips through me. *Why does this bother me?*

I glance at them, and Parker looks my way. I scowl at him, then turn and grab some drinks. I take them to the nearest fridge, open the door, and load it up.

My skin prickles as I sense someone behind me. "Hey, little mouse. Can I get one of those grape energy drinks?"

Parker's warm breath tickles my ear. It startles me that he's so close, yet a warmth spreads through me.

I spin around, and we come face-to-face.

"Do you mind?" I gesture at his closeness.

His playful grin is spread across his features, but he takes a tiny step back. He's wearing a red basketball jersey and baggy shorts. Those arms are out on full display again. Shaking my head, I turn and grab the drink he's after.

"You didn't seem to mind my closeness the other night." His eyebrows raise in question, and I hate myself for allowing him to get close that way. Of course, he's using it against me.

"Screw you, Parker. You saw an opportunity to swoop in and play a hero. I was drunk and don't recall much of it anyway. Sorry to disappoint you." I shrug, squeezing past him to go ring up his order. I attempt not to touch him, but I fail. He has no sense of boundaries.

"Would you like a refresher?" His fingers graze my bare arm.

I pick my pace up to escape his fiery touch. I'm so annoyed at myself for feeling like this toward him. He brings a mixture of emotions out in me, some I don't want to experience. He's such an arrogant ass. I have to keep reminding myself of the vow I made to steer clear of guys like him and Hayden. "You have some nerve. You've got a date here, and you're hitting on me," I whisper to him across the counter.

He merely shrugs and turns his head to eye Barbie at the table. She leans forward, pushing out her boobs and giving him a flirtatious smile.

"What's a bit of fun?"

Even though I know he's playing with me, it rubs me the wrong way. My defenses go up when I'm around Parker. I'm so afraid of letting someone like him in and getting hurt all over again, so instead, I become a bitch. Perhaps keeping him at arm's length would be for the best. Although how do I not let these feelings I have toward Parker affect me?

"Yeah, and what are people's feelings to you?

Nothing? Maybe you should think about that before hitting on me while taking someone else on a date."

He says nothing, but slides some money across the counter. I hand him his change with trembling hands. They betray me.

Parker stands there, watching me. He's unreadable. It jolts my nerves even more. Leaning across the counter, he says, "Little mouse, there's so much that you don't know. I'm not locked down with you or anyone. I was also burned, and this is how I deal with things. It's me. I flirt. People know who I am, but who are you? Think about that."

Turning on his heel, he takes on his jock of a persona, flirting. Barbie's giggle fills the café.

Parker's words rock me. *Who am I?*

I've lost track of who I am and became the follower. I followed Hayden like a little puppy. My chest tightens, and tears swell in my eyes. I race to the storeroom, swiping them away. I don't want Parker to see how he affects me.

The counter bell rings. I straighten up my shirt and wipe my face, clearing it of any trace of moisture. Smoothing down my clothes, I walk out the front, except it's not Parker. Hayden's standing there with a bunch of flowers.

Is he kidding himself?

My gaze shifts to where Parker is sitting, and he looks up at Hayden with such a hate-filled gaze. I hope they don't get into another fight right here.

"Can I help you, Hayden? Sorry, we don't sell wine here. If you're after a bottle to take and meet up with Ella, that is."

Hayden's head hangs low. "I wanted to apologize for the other night. These are for you." He places the bunch of yellow roses on the bench in front of me. They're beautiful, half open, and an intense and sweet-smelling fragrance pours from them.

Folding my arms across my chest to shield myself, I say, "I accept your apology. Thank you."

Hayden nods, simply standing there. He doesn't make any move to turn and leave.

"Is there something else?" I may sound confident, however inside I'm a bundle of nerves. I know what this guy is like, and he has the shortest of tempers. Like the other day, when he was saying sorry yet again, and then it was like a switch flipped in him and the next minute, his temper was flaring.

Hayden picks something off his shirt; I'm not sure anything was there though. "I wanted to say you were right about Ella. I really want us to give things another go. I'm sorry for my outbursts and the unkind words I said. I can't help it."

I'm numb to his words and emotions. I couldn't care less.

Parker's question comes burning back into my thoughts. *Who am I?*

I'm not some stupid girl who'll fall for this sorry excuse of a man. How many times can one person say sorry, then treat that same person like a piece of dirt under their shoes? And then have the guts to come and ask for yet another chance?

"Thanks for your apology, but things between us are completely over. There's no chance of us ever getting back together. We aren't right for each other." Those words ring true. We're complete opposites.

Hayden says nothing. Instead, he turns and leaves the café.

My head drops. A sigh of relief expels from my lungs.

"Are you all right?"

My head flicks up, and Parker's concerned face stares back at me. "It's not any of your concern, Parker. Enjoy your date. We close in ten minutes."

"Don't shut me out, little mouse." There's no humor in his words, yet there is care and concern.

Squaring my shoulders, I say, "I never let you in in the first place, so I'm not shutting you out. You're just someone who shared an experience with me. We were both cheated on. Enjoy your night, Parker."

I turn my back on him and begin my close-up duties. I try my hardest to keep my head down and not acknowledge him again. I'm highly aware of his stare following me around the room as I stack the chairs and pack up the tables.

Five minutes later, Barbie leaves, and it's just Parker and me in the store with Jen out the back. He begins helping me by stacking the tables and chairs.

"I don't need your help. This is my job."

"I know, but I want to help."

I don't want to argue with him, so I let him wipe over the tables while I finish stacking drinks in the fridge.

When we finish, Jen comes out. "Oh, thank you for helping," she gushes at Parker, who smiles and assures her it's nothing, and that he's happy to help.

I grab my stuff from the back office and head out the front door. "See you later, Jen. Don't stay too late now."

She laughs and shuts the door after Parker, and I exit.

Turning toward my building, I say, "See ya later. Thanks for helping me."

Parker quickly moves around in front of me, blocking my passage.

"I don't have time for this." I sigh.

"Sorry about before."

I curse. "Parker, I'm so sick of hearing that damn word. It's run its course. I'm tired of people saying sorry to me and wanting another chance. Am I that easy people think they can walk all over me?" I yell. A lump has formed in my throat, and I'm not sure if I want to cry or scream.

Parker stands there, his eyes don't leave mine.

"What? Are you just going to stand there, watching me lose my mind? You asked if I knew who I was... maybe I don't. There! Are you happy?" Wetness cools my cheeks. *Perfect!*

Stepping around Parker, I'm about to run. I need to run.

He grabs my wrist, and before I realize what's going on, he's wrapped me up in his arms. He holds me against his chest while each tear drops onto his shirt. I don't fight him. Instead, I revel in his calmness, comfort, and support.

When Parker holds me, his arms encase me so tightly I feel like I'm being shielded from the outside world. It's as if I'm wearing a suit of armor. He lets me fall apart and doesn't say a word. When eventually everything I have been holding onto has been erased, frustrations and hurt over Hayden and Ella, and even the annoyance I'd felt toward Parker has dwindled, a sense of peace comes over me.

After some time, I step back. I can't bring myself to make eye contact with him. I say two simple words, "Thank you."

I don't allow him to speak. Instead, I turn and run back to my room without stopping. He probably thinks I'm pathetic, some broken girl who wants his attention or something.

CHAPTER
Twelve

It's been a week since I've spoken to Parker. I've avoided him like the plague. I'm not sure what my emotions are telling me lately. One thing I know for sure is that they're not siding with my head, which is telling me to guard myself.

I can still feel Parker's arms around me. I close my eyes at night, and I'm there with him again as he pulls me against his warm body. I can still smell his spicy scent. It's crazy how the mind works.

It's nearly closing time on Monday, and he hasn't made an appearance. Maybe he took my hint and has decided to keep away from me. He didn't even message me, which stung.

Why does he get to me so much?

Picking my phone up from the bench, I see there's a message from Elsie.

Elsie: So... has Monday night guy shown up?

Monday night guy? I'm confused by her message.

Addison: Was that for me?

Elsie: Yes.

Now, I'm more confused than ever.

Addison: Who's Monday night guy?

I watch the three dots bounce as I wait for her reply to come through.

Elsie: Parker, silly.

Addison: What's with the nickname?

Elsie: Well, he comes in like clockwork every Monday night. It seems to fit. Don't ya think?

Addison: Fair enough. No, he hasn't come in.

Elsie: Yet... you should just give him a chance.

Give him a chance? Who is she kidding?

Muffled voices come from outside the café. Looking up, I see Parker and Stacey outside. I perch up on my chair, trying to zone in on what they're saying. I can't take my eyes off them. Parker has a scowl on his face. I can't see Stacey's face clearly enough to know what's going on with her. She's using her hands a lot and being very expressive. One hand comes up and swipes at her cheek. *Is she crying?*

Parker reaches out and takes her hand, pulling her into his arms. My stomach hardens. So this is a regular thing for him? To comfort every girl who cries in front of him?

Turmoil builds inside my stomach. I can't believe this is happening. I shouldn't care. He's nothing to me. No one.

Turning my back on the scene, I decide the storeroom needs cleaning. Instead of cleaning, I sit in there and switch the light off.

Sitting in the darkness is soothing. There's nothing and no one I can see or hear. No one to analyze my expressions. I take some deep breaths, trying to loosen my hardened stomach.

The bell above the door rings. I already know who it's going to be. I have to face him, and I'm not sure I can.

Gathering up some courage, I finally step out of the room and pass through the doorway, and I'm standing face-to-face with Parker. His head is down; he's digging through his sports bag. Time to suck it up.

Taking a breath, I plaster a smile on my face. "Hey. Just the drink?"

Parker's head springs up when I speak. A breathtaking smile lights up his face. My body begins to tremble.

"Hey, little mouse. Yeah. Thanks." He extends his hand with the change in it. I open my shaking hand, and he drops his money into it. His fingers graze my palm. Tingles shoot up my arm and ignite my heart. My body reacts to his like a lightning bolt. His touch jolts me, so I quickly pull my hand away and finish processing his order. I expect him to leave, only he doesn't. He stands at the counter, watching me.

"Do you want something else?" I treat him like I would any other customer. After seeing him cuddle Stacey, I'm not sure I want to get close to him again and allow myself to get hurt. I can't do it.

He eyes me, tilting his head to the side. "Something's bothering you."

"No, it's not," I answer much too quickly.

He raises his eyebrows. "I don't believe it." He places his drink in his bag.

"Well, if there's something bothering me, I'm not about to tell you now, because apparently, you hug every girl who cries in front of you." The words spew from my mouth almost too quickly, and it's too late now for me to retract what I've said. *Damn my big mouth.*

His mouth forms an O shape. "This is about what you saw out front, huh?"

This time, I decide not saying anything. I simply shrug.

"Aren't I allowed to comfort someone?"

"Do whatever you want. It's your life; it's got nothing to do with me." I keep my face neutral so I don't give away my emotions.

"Then why are you so huffy over me hugging Stacey?" he questions.

"I'm not huffy," I scoff, crossing my arms over my chest. "I think you'd better be careful, and that's all I'm saying. You do what you want, though."

"Good. I will. I'll message you later." He turns his back on me, and I'm left speechless.

CHAPTER
Thirteen

I t's been an entire week since I witnessed Parker holding Stacey in his arms. Like a skillful ninja, I've managed to steer clear of him again. I'm becoming good at it. He hasn't bothered to message me. I can't believe him.

In English, I've made sure I sat between two people who were already seated. And even though we've been partnered for an assignment, it hasn't been given yet, so I'm in the clear… for now.

Jen pops her head out from the back area. "You can start packing up, Addison. Finish up early."

I pick up the washcloth and spray to clean. "All right, Jen."

I haven't flipped the sign to 'closed' since technically, we're not. I put some music on my cell phone and play it through the shop's sound system. It helps me get the job done quicker.

My watch beeps at the hour. I go and lock the door and flip the sign, then turn off the outside lights. When I look back out the glass windows, Parker's standing there, and a scream erupts from my throat.

Jen comes flying into the room. "What's wrong? Are you okay?" She takes hold of my shoulders, giving me the once-over as I clutch my chest.

"Yes, sorry." I point outside where Parker is bending over, laughing. "He sc-scared me."

"Oh, thank goodness. You scared me. If he needs something, let him grab it." She lets go of me, and unlocks the door. My legs feel like Jell-O. If I move, I'm afraid I might collapse in a puddle on the floor. My heart rate still hasn't gone back to a normal rhythm.

Parker walks through the door. He and Jen speak.

"You okay there, little mouse? Didn't mean to frighten you." He claps me on the back, and humor pours from his words.

"Sure you didn't," I say dryly. I shift out of his grasp and get back to my job while Jen serves Parker.

Picking up another chair, I peek up at him. He's wearing a maroon and gold River Valley College basketball jersey. Obviously, he comes here after practice. Of course.

"Hey, Addison?"

My name leaving his mouth causes my stomach to twist into knots. I don't want to feel like this around him. This attraction I have has to be because we share something in common. Yes, that's what it is. That's why my emotions are all up in arms.

I can totally keep him at a distance.

Heck, who am I trying to reassure?

Stopping what I'm doing, I lift my head right up. His piercing stare stabs me right in the heart. There's no trace of humor on his face anymore. This is serious, sensitive Parker standing before me. Right now, I'd give anything for it to be the jerk Parker so I could continue to convince myself he was a player and just like Hayden.

Who am I kidding?

"Yes?" I reply as I brush a loose hair that's fallen from my ponytail out of my face.

"Just wanted to check on you. See how you've been." He plays with the top of his energy drink as he stands there. *Is he nervous?* I want to block out those who I'm afraid might hurt me. Parker's one of the most popular guys in college, known for his skills on the court and in the bedroom. He's bedded a fair few girls, from what I've heard. He's a player. Everyone knows it. And now that he's single, I'm sure he's taking advantage of that fact.

"It hasn't worried you lately, so why should it now?" My guard goes up. It's my new defense mechanism.

"What's that supposed to mean?" he bites out. He stands up straighter, clearly annoyed at what I've said.

"Is your phone broken?"

"No."

"So you say you'll message me and don't?"

Realization registers on his face. His eyes turn cold. "What, so you can ignore me, and yet I'm the one who's always in the wrong? I don't get you, Addison. It's like nothing is good enough for you. Yeah, I let you have your space. It's not like you're my girlfriend; I don't need to check on you. Sorry." His words slice through me with what feels like a jagged knife.

"Glad we got that out of the way. See ya." I turn my

back to him. The bell chimes as the door opens and swings shut, and I'm once again left speechless.

Maybe I am the issue.

Maybe I'm the one with the problem.

When I finish up, Jen lets me out. The night's clear; I can see a few stars in the sky and a big bright full moon. It's the perfect night to shoot some hoops, and I need a release. I race back to the dorm, quickly change, and grab the basketball from my cupboard, along with a water bottle. I take off to the basketball court to clear my head.

I enter the basketball building. It's quiet. Lights fill the arena. I look around; it appears no one is here. *Fantastic!* Placing my water bottle down, I bounce the ball, and it echoes around the room. I stand at the three-pointer line and shoot. Shot after shot goes in.

"Why didn't you try out for the girls' team?"

I spin around. Parker stands there with a ball tucked under his arm.

I shrug, turning back toward the ring and taking another shot. Damn it. This time I miss. "Basketball isn't my life. When I was younger, Dad and I would mess around a fair bit, and it was good because Devon, my brother, became attached to the game and he's even better than me." I remember Devon trying again and again to get the ball in the hoop. His determination's phenomenal. I'm sure he could easily get into college and play basketball.

Parker stands across from me on the line, taking shots and, of course, not missing any. I can't help myself; I watch him. The muscles in his arms flex, and when he goes to take the shot, he jumps a little. Even though it's a small jump, when he lands his muscles tense, defining his physique.

"Want a game of one-on-one?" he asks as he releases another shot.

Already knowing he's going to win, I figure, why not? "Sure. First to five wins?"

"Yeah, but I have other stipulations."

This isn't going to end well for me. "What are they?"

He's silent for a moment. "If I win, you have to be nice to me. Stop assuming I'm some jackass—"

"I thought that was what you were?" I cut in. Innocence chimes in my tone.

Parker chuckles and holds his hand up to stop me from continuing. "I wasn't finished, little mouse."

"Go on, hot shot."

"Now, as I was saying, you have to be nice to me, and you have to let me take you out."

I eye him skeptically. Is this some joke or trick to get back at Stacey or Hayden? I'm not in the market for revengeful dating. In fact, I should stick to my decision not to date guys like him. "Sorry, I can't do the date. I've decided to refrain from the dating scene."

"Well, don't look at it as a date then. It'll just be two friends heading out." The last part of his sentence causes my stomach to plummet. *Friends.* He takes another shot, then holds the ball. His stare grips me, and somehow, I find myself nodding in agreement to his terms.

"What if I win?"

Parker erupts with laughter. "Don't worry, little mouse. I'll be sure to at least let you get one shot in," he teases.

"Bring it on." I place my ball down beside my water. I can feel the smile on my face—it's one I haven't worn in a long time. It's as if there's a brightness coming from within me. I love sports, but I've never really done anything with it, never joined a team. I know I'm sure to lose against the basketball captain, but what's a bit of fun?

Parker tosses the ball to me. "Here, you can start. It might be the only shot I allow you to have. I'll take it easy on you."

"Not too easy, I hope," I respond playfully. A smile that I'm sure mimics my own sits on Parker's face.

"Stop stalling," he says. I take a sneaky advantage.

I dribble the ball to the hoop. Parker comes toward me. I balk him to go one way, and instead, I go the other. He's back on me within seconds. I hit the three-point line and take the shot. I don't miss.

"Lucky shot."

I toss the ball to him. He takes it back out to halfway then comes driving back in, only he's coming right at me. I don't move. Instead, I hold my arms out, and when he comes near I manage a sneaky tap on the ball and collect it from him. "Watch out there, Parker. You might just lose to a girl." I laugh before running in, dribbling the ball.

Parker wraps his arms around me, stealing the ball. I become warm. My body craves his touch. He's lit it up, and now my stupid body is betraying me. Yet again.

Parker releases me and dribbles the ball away, I say, "You can't do that. I call foul ball." Before I register what's happening, Parker's taken a shot, and through the hoop it goes.

"I'll give you two foul shots then. Here," he says.

I catch the ball he tosses me. I align myself on the foul shot line. Parker comes around from behind me. He's stripped his jersey off. It appears the gods decided they would give him a body like theirs—one of pure perfection. *He won't get to me,* I chant in my mind. I give my head a shake and keep my focus on the job at hand: kicking his ass.

Parker's heat hits my back. My senses light up like a Christmas tree. A finger slides down my arm. I swallow the hard lump in my throat. Each and every part of me wants to turn and plant a kiss on his lips. I must refrain. It's like the devil tempting Eve all over again. Parker's lips are the most forbidden fruit.

I bounce the ball twice, bending slightly to take one of my two free shots. My ass hits his crotch. Parker's hands land on my hips seconds later.

Oh, he's so good at this. What a tease.

But two can play at this game.

CHAPTER
Fourteen

With his hand burning through the material of my tights, I lean back so my butt is pushed against him. I collide with something completely unexpected, Parker's heated body. It shocks me enough to encourage me to take my shot. It goes in.

"Good shot," he breathes against the tender skin under my ear. It sends an electrifying current through my entire chest.

I shrug, not saying anything. I bend my knees again, preparing to line up my second shot. Parker's hands wrap around my waist, pulling me into him, and my breath leaves me.

"Breathe," his tantalizing voice whispers against my neck. I obey, only my chest feels as though there's a weight resting on it. "Take your next shot, little mouse." He chuckles, then releases me. I don't want him to.

Standing upright, I take my second shot and don't miss. I turn around and drink up his six-pack. "I think you might lose, Parker." I run my index finger down his bare chest teasingly.

Parker steps closer. "We'll see about that." He leaves me standing there speechless and goes to retrieve the ball.

After about five minutes, we're tied, three all. This is a game of teaser basketball. If he has the ball, I do my best to distract him in some way, like standing in front of him while cupping my breast. It doesn't faze him.

The next two points are scored, and we're still tied. "You can play a good game, little mouse, but can you really beat the captain of the basketball team? You do realize I'm taking it easy on you."

"If you say so." My lips twist up, keen to see how he plays this next round. I have something planned he won't see coming.

He dribbles the ball out to halfway and comes back in. I stand in his path, just before the three-pointer shot clearance.

When he gets closer, he sees me coming at him. He goes to take a shot from out farther. I run at him. "Catch me," I shout, as I leap and hope to goodness he catches me. The ball leaves his hands immediately, and then his arms wrap securely around my body. He collapses under me.

Sitting up, I turn my head. The ball goes through the hoop. *Damn him.*

Slowly, I register that Parker's under me. I rest on my knees, one on either side of Parker's hips. "Oh, sorry." I go to stand, but his hands hold me there. I don't fight against his grip; I revel in it instead.

"Looks like I'm taking you out, and now you have to

be nice to me." His piercing stare pins me in place. My heart pumps erratically, and my hands shake.

"I really thought my little trick would have thrown you a bit."

"It did. I didn't expect that last ball to go in. I had to catch you; I couldn't let you fall." His thumb makes gentle circles on my hip. Those words, *I couldn't let you fall,* are powerful. Perhaps he's not the kind of guy I think he is.

"I should get off you. Me and all my sweaty goodness is a little gross." I release a nervous laugh. Even though I say I should get up, I don't budge. His grip and lust-filled eyes glue me to him. His hand moves up my back, applying pressure, encouraging me to lean down on his bare chest. *Oh, my hell, what is happening?*

My body responds to his caress. I find myself leaning into him. Parker licks his lips. *Is he going to kiss me? Do I want to be kissed?*

"Don't worry, little mouse. I won't try anything, I only want to hold you."

"But I'm icky."

"I don't care. I am as well." At those words, I surrender to him. I lay against his chest, and I can hear his heart going crazy. It sounds as wild as mine feels.

Am I dreaming? I'm lying on the floor of the basketball court in Parker Kent's arms. I must have lost the plot.

Nothing but the sound of our breathing fills the room until Parker shuffles beneath me. I raise off him. I'm not sure how long we've lain there, but it was probably the only time in the last two weeks when I've actually felt some peace settle within me. I go to stand. Again, he stops me. He holds me, pressing his head against my chest.

"Just wanted a hug, hey?" I say jokingly.

He nudges his head against my boob. "Little mouse,

you were teasing me, so I think this is the most restraint I can muster. In a perfect world, my hand would be cupping these cushions."

I break out with laughter. "You filthy guy." I playfully shove his arm. After a moment, I decide it's time to end this. Whatever this is. "Well, I better get going. The court will be closing soon."

This time he lets me up, and he jumps to his feet effortlessly. "Wanna go another round tomorrow night?"

I think about his proposition. A part of me wants to leap at him again, and this time crush my lips to his. *Would he kiss me back?*

"Umm… I'll let you know. I think I'm supposed to do something tomorrow night with Elsie."

"Elsie? Is that your loud friend from the party?"

"That's the one."

Parker slips his jersey over his god-like body. I pick up my water bottle, taking three full mouthfuls. When I look up, Parker's standing there with his hand out. I hand him my drink, and he sculls the remainder of it.

"I like her. She says it how it is." He's spot on about Elsie.

"Yes, that's one of the many reasons I love her."

We grab the basketball, and exit the court and stand outside. There's a cool breeze, which makes the sweat on my skin much cooler.

"How are you going with things after Hayden?" His question throws me, and I immediately screw up my face.

"I don't want to talk about him, or Stacey, or even Ella." It's in the past now.

"Actually, I wanted to ask what the deal was with you and your sister."

"That falls into the, I don't really want to talk about it. Sorry."

As we walk, Parker places his arm over my shoulders. Being close to him drives me crazy, but in a good way. As much as I want to push him away, he always comes back and keeps trying.

"When's your first game of the season?" I ask, wanting to change the subject.

"Why? You wanna come cheer me on?" He pulls me tighter against him. We stroll past the darkened classroom buildings and a couple of other students. There are gasps from some when they see Parker. One girl I recognize instantly—*Barbie*. She spots us and bounces over to us, her ponytail swinging side to side. She's wearing gym clothes as well.

"Hey, Parker, baby. I was looking for you." Her eyes land where Parker's arm rests, and he drops it immediately. I look up at him. Why did he do that? Is he worried about being caught with me?

I decide to leave him be. I don't want to make this awkward for either of us. "All right, Kent, good game. I'll see ya... maybe tomorrow." I rest my hand on his bicep, giving a little squeeze. He tenses under my touch.

Parker rakes his hand through his hair as if he's unsure of what he's going to do. I turn away from them and make my way back to the dorm. I'll admit it stung he didn't turn Barbie away. But like he said, we're not together, so I've got nothing to be jealous about. I can't help it, though. He's brought some feelings of want to the surface. Perhaps it's best if I pack them away for another time.

As I walk, I remember our kiss from last year. Parker had been trying to get close to me all night. I wasn't sure what his game was at the time. As our lips had locked, it was as if the party around us had faded away.

I've thought nothing of it up until now. I know Hayden and I were never going to last a lifetime; I never felt like that when I kissed him. Kissing Hayden was nothing like it felt with Parker.

"So where were you last night?" Elsie bounces up beside me, hooking her arm through mine as we walk to our next class.

"Went to the basketball courts and had a game of one-on-one with Parker," I reply with a tone of 'it's nothing to fuss about.' Elsie, on the other hand, grips my arm with both her hands, jumps up and down squealing at me. I swear she might rip my arm from its socket. Of course, she's excited.

"OMG… O.M.G. Tell me everything! Did you win?" Elsie knows about my basketball ability; she learned the hard way. Same as she did with Devon.

I laugh at her enthusiasm. "You do realize we're just what you would call 'sometimes friends.'" *If you can even call us that.*

"Yeah, I don't care. I want details."

I glance at her. She eyes me. Her excitement level is off the charts. I think she really would like to see the outcome of what might or could happen between Parker and me. I also think she'd like to rub whatever this is between Parker and I in Hayden's face.

"All right, well, we played a game of one-on-one basketball. That's about it." I shrug while receiving an evil glare from Elsie. Her face says, *'You're kidding me, right?'*

"Come on. Don't give me the watered-down version."

"There was some flirting—that was to distract each other so we'd miss our shots. I even, at one point, threw myself at him to catch me so he wouldn't get the ball in. It failed." I giggle, remembering the moment.

I feel Elsie's stare at me and await her onslaught. "You actually threw your body at him?"

I nod.

She tugs my arm, stopping us from walking. "Did anything else happen?"

"No. Like I said, it was just a game between friends."

Elsie rolls her eyes, but the dirty look on her face isn't for me—it's for whoever's standing behind me. I get a waft of a very familiar perfume. The flowery scent hits my nostrils, and I rub my nose as it itches. Spinning around, I see Ella's standing there, her friends close behind her. My mouth drops open at the sight of Devon standing beside her. She pushes him toward me. When I catch him, his body trembles under my touch.

"Devon, what are you doing here?" I grip his face to make him look at me. When he does, I can see a pinkness on his cheeks as though someone has hit him. My insides light up like an inferno. I whip my head toward Ella. "What happened to him?" I grit out through my teeth. My goodness, I want to slap her to the ground. If she's hurt him, I will harm that bitch.

Ella simply laughs in my face. "I didn't do anything. He showed up here asking around for you. Deal with it." She turns her back on me and struts away, her posse following closely behind her.

"What a bunch of bitches." Elsie throws the word 'bitches' loudly at them. They don't turn around. Elsie knows how protective I am of Devon, she's met him a couple of times before.

I wrap my arm around my brother's shoulders. He's bulkier than me, but he's like a little child, and he has tears in his eyes and red marks not only on his face but his arms. I lead him away from onlookers who'll only sit and laugh at him. Some people can't look past his disability.

"What happened, Devon?" I ask gently as we sit under a tree on campus, away from the busy lunchtime pathways.

I watch him tap away at his knee, and my heart breaks. Tears burn in my eyes. Damn, I hate people.

"I… I… It was those boys. The ones Mom spoke to the school about."

I suck in a hard breath and hear Elsie curse a heap of times under her breath. I hold Devon tightly against me. His body still shakes. That's it. I'm done with petty kids.

"I'm going to the school myself and talking with these stupid boys."

Devon's head flicks up, and he shakes it profusely. "No, Addy… they're the top boys of the school." Devon taps away on his knee. *Tap, tap, tap.*

"Something has to be done about this," I clip. I pull out my cell to call Mom and Dad. Mom should be at home today.

My phone's snatched from my shaky grip. "Hey," I begin, but stop when I look up to see Parker, Jimmy, and Dane standing above us. "What are you doing?" I quickly wipe away the wetness on my cheeks. A soft look on Parker's face settles the anger and hurt hurtling through me.

"We want to help," he says.

"How do you even know what's going on? This doesn't concern you anyway."

"I overheard what was going on. We've got this," Parker says with a sternness that tells me he means business.

CHAPTER Fifteen

"No, Parker. I can't let you do this." I chase after him and his duo. Jimmy gives me a sideways glance. I can't tell if he dislikes me or not now. That day he ran me over, I could have sworn he hated my guts.

"As Parker said… we've got this." I stop in my tracks. *Is he really defending my brother?* There's a seriousness to his words, just like Parker's from moments ago.

Devon comes up beside me, and I take his hand. "Stop!" Devon yells with such confidence it shocks me. He's not one to normally raise his voice.

It stops the boys in their tracks. They turn and look back at Elsie, Devon, and me.

"No one should be treated how he has been." Parker points to Devon, who's back to tapping, more like hitting his upper leg. I can see the bruises forming on his cheek.

"Those little dickwads need a lesson taught to them,"

Parker says. Jimmy and Dane nod in agreement, they all turn and leave. "You can either come with us or stay here. It's your choice."

I look sideways at Devon. He's already started taking off after Parker.

I rub my hands down my face, exhausted by all of this. I don't want others to get in trouble for my family. I turn to Elsie. "I'll go with them. I'll fill you in later."

Elsie pushes me away. "Yes, you better. Now get going, or they'll leave without you."

I take off running. My legs carry me across the pathways. The boys are men on a mission, and seem to have strides like giants. I finally catch up with them. Devon glances at me and takes my hand. I catch Parker looking at me, our gazes lock briefly before he turns away. It settles the fueling fire that's been lit inside me.

We arrive in the parking lot. Parker opens one of the back doors of a navy blue Jeep Wrangler. Devon jumps in and puts himself in the middle. I go to slide in beside him, and Parker grips my hand, giving it a gentle squeeze. My chest flutters at his touch. Seconds later, he releases me and hops in the front while I finish sliding into the car.

Devon's caught the exchange between Parker and me. The smile on his face is a dead giveaway.

"Where to?" Parker asks once we're all piled in the Jeep.

"River Valley High School," I say.

Parker takes off. Music pulses through the sound system. Dane is sitting in the back with Devon and me. Dane isn't one who usually says much, from what I've noticed, yet he leans into Devon and says, "I'm Dane." He holds out his hand for Devon to shake.

Devon looks down at it. "Devon." He grips Dane's hand in his.

"You all right?" Dane asks, gently.

Devon's head drops low, and he begins tapping his right leg again. I take his hand to comfort him. "I'm all right. It's not the first time this has happened, but... but today they picked on Tommy as well, and he pretended to be sick so he could go home." Oh my goodness. That poor boy. I want to wrap both him and my brother in cotton wool and never let them out of my sight.

I hear Parker curse, and I look up. He catches my now watery gaze. His hard stare holds mine.

I look back to Devon who's still talking to Dane, only now they're chatting about basketball and threatening to beat each other. Devon's laughter fills the interior of the car and brings a smile to my face.

Five minutes later, we pull up outside of Devon's school, and his hold on my hand tightens. "I don't want to go back in," Devon says in a low whisper. His hands shake. I want to run in and beat the hell out of the kids who've hurt my brother and his friend. Thankfully, Devon's holding me back.

"You don't have to. I'll take you home after this, and we can let Mom know what's happened, if she doesn't already," I say. He slowly bobs his head up and down, acknowledging what I've said.

Parker turns in his seat. "What are the boys' names?" His kindness toward Devon turns what hardness is left of my defenses to jelly.

Devon raises his hand, pointing his finger out the windshield. All our focus shifts to where he's pointing. A group of four teenage boys stand around the side of a building, looking as if they're trying to skip out on school. *What little punks.*

"Let's go, boys." There's a playfulness to Parker's sentence. This could be interesting.

All three of the trio roll out of the car. It's like a scene you'd see in a movie—all three step from the car as if in slow-motion. Well, maybe it's not exactly like that. It sure feels like it, though.

Devon and I slide from the car much more slowly. The boys haven't waited. They've set their scowls of hatred on their targets and have gone for them. Devon and I take off to catch up.

A boy sees us approaching. A creepy smile spreads across his face as he taps his friends on the shoulder, and they all make their way toward us.

Parker, Jimmy, and Dane stop in their tracks. The younger boys halt a few feet in front of our group.

"Oh, little Devy has brought some backup. Can't handle it, huh?" All four of them laugh. *Are these guys not even fazed about Parker and his friends being here?*

I barge between Parker and Jimmy, stopping in front of the dick-bag ringleader. "Who do you think you are, picking on my brother?"

Dick-bag's laugher tips fuel onto my fire, which is already raging. I shove him in the chest. He stumbles back but squares his shoulders, and his mates' glares are like daggers in my direction. "Be careful, little girl. This isn't your school. We run this joint."

Now, it's my turn to laugh in their faces.

"Now, now don't go threatening her," Parker says. I sense him standing right behind me.

"And who are you?" Dick-bag spits.

"I'm Parker, and these are my friends Jimmy and Dane." Parker rests his hands on my shoulders, gently moving me out of the way and placing me protectively behind him and the boys. Devon comes to stand with me. There's amusement resting on his features. He doesn't look worried at the outcome of this at all while Parker continues, "We're from a college not far from here."

His eyes go wide as recognition dawns on Dick-bag's face.

"So what?" he asks. Yet, I can tell that he's a little more nervous than cocky now.

Parker steps up into him, getting right up into Dick-bag's face. "If I find out you've hurt my friend's brother again, I'll be back, and you'll be the one leaving with more than one shiner on your face." The sternness of his voice would make any kid scared. I felt the anger with each word he spoke. I want to high-five him.

"It's none of your business what happens here."

This guy doesn't give up. Probably wants to appear the big dog while his mates are around.

"Oh, I'm making it my business. You see, Devon's sister is a good friend of mine, and when you hurt him, you're hurting her. Which means next time it happens I'll be hurting you, and your buddies."

"He's a freak." Dick-bag stabs his finger at Devon, who drops his head, and I spot his tear falling.

That's it.

I storm up to Dick-bag. Stepping in front of Parker and the boys, I shove the loser back, and I push him again. Rage fuels me on. I want to cause him pain—worse pain than what he's caused Devon. "How dare you? You're a... pathetic. Little. Boy."

He keeps stepping back, I clench my fist and swing it at his face. The pain which seers through my hand and shoots up my arm tells me I've done something to it, but it doesn't stop me.

Dick-bag holds his hand to his face, then comes at me with his arms out.

"Oh, I wouldn't do th—"

Parker's warning is too late. I've gripped the Dick-bag's arm with my good hand and turned into him like I did with Parker a few weeks back. In one swift move, I have Dick-bag on his back.

I stare down at him, flat on his back. A swirl of excitement pumps through my veins. He looks up at me, his mouth hanging open.

"Leave my brother alone or me and my friends here will be back." I turn toward Parker, Jimmy, Dane, and Devon. Each of them has the biggest of smiles on their faces.

"I like her," Jimmy says, nudging Parker. Devon chuckles to himself, and Dane gives him a slap on the back. "Your sister is badass, Dev," he says.

Devon nods excitedly. "She's the best," he gloats.

Parker's blue eyes settle on me. "She sure is."

My body heats, and my pulse speeds up.

We arrive back at the college around two in the afternoon. My hand still throbs from hitting Dick-bag. When he scurried to his feet after I dropped him, he and his buddies took off quickly.

"Come on, Devon. I'll take you home," I say as we climb out of the Jeep. I shut my door, and Parker stands there, leaning against his closed door.

"Did you want me to take him?" he asks.

Before I can answer, Devon voices his opinion. "Yes, I like your car."

Shrugging, I say, "Well, I guess Devon has answered for me."

Jimmy and Dane come from behind the car. "Thanks for your help, guys."

Jimmy shrugs. "Not that we did much." He gives me a crooked smile. He actually looks good when he does it. All he'd need to say is 'How you doing?' and the girls would flock to him. Unfortunately, he acts like a clown a majority of the time.

"Happy to help Dev out," Dane says clapping Devon on the back. My brother's entire face lights up. I can tell he really likes Dane.

"Th-Thank you," Devon stutters. He hasn't been tapping as much as he was when he first arrived. That tells me that he's in a happy place and is calm.

"We'll have to have a game… one-on-one, hey, Dev?" Parker asks.

Devon nods furiously with excitement. "Yes. When?"

"Give him a date and time so he can know and be prepared," I say, giving Parker a knowing look. Devon is very much into routine. He likes to have warning for things. If he doesn't, sometimes, he can't handle it, although he's much better at controlling his emotions now that he's older.

"Monday night. I can pick you up. It won't be until after nine p.m; that way Addy can come. What do you say?"

"Yes, sounds good," Devon says. I can see the excitement shining through him.

"I'll let Mom and Dad know for you," I say.

"I wanna watch," Dane says, and Jimmy nods his interest as well.

"Sounds good. Well, better get Dev home," Parker says, clapping a hand on Jimmy and Dane's shoulders. This was an outcome I didn't expect.

Parker, Devon, and I slide back into the Jeep, and I give the driver our address.

Parker stares at me. "What's with the look?" he asks.

"What do you mean?" I ask as I buckle myself in.

"What's with the look?"

"What look?" I have no idea what he's referring to.

"You look surprised?"

My face must read as shocked after Jimmy actually said goodbye to me.

"I guess I'm a little surprised at Jimmy and how nice he's being to me."

Parker laughs beside me. "I had words with him."

"What?" I practically shout, twisting toward him. "Why would you do that?"

"He likes you," a voice sings happily from the backseat, answering instead of Parker. I feel the heat on my cheeks. Damn Devon and his lack of filter. "I like him better than Hayden. He was a loser."

I cover my face, laughing. I can hear the snickers from beside me, and I peek out between my fingers to look at Parker. He stares ahead, watching the road. There's a grin on his face. *How embarrassing.*

I love Devon.

I drop my hands back into my lap.

"I get the feeling you never miss anything, Dev?" Parker asks with a hint of humor to his question.

"Nope," Devon answers with a pop on the P. "You like her, don't you?"

Silence fills the car. Parker goes mute, and I steal a glance at him. His arms are tense as he grips the steering wheel. I watch his jaw tick, and I can tell he's deep in thought. I thought he'd respond with something like 'yeah, I like her as a friend.' I'm fine with being friend-zoned. He's Parker Kent, and there are heaps of girls who want him, myself included. Not that I would admit that to anyone if it meant getting death stares from other girls at school.

"Well?" Devon pushes. I'm secretly glad he does, because there's a part of me that wants to know Parker's thoughts.

He looks in his rearview mirror, and says. "Perhaps I better talk to Addison about it first."

"Yeah okay, but don't break her heart."

A simple sentence holds so much power.

CHAPTER

Sixteen

We dropped Devon home and I explained to Mom why he was there. She wasn't impressed that she didn't get called. I had to tell her I'd handled it, and not in a conventional way. Devon informed us that he'd ran from school to college. He should have just rang me and I would have come.

Mom doesn't miss much, and she could see my hand was swollen. I swear she grinned; it was gone within seconds though. She can be hard to get through to sometimes, but I love her.

"Get your hand checked," was all she said on the matter.

Parker won over my mother. Even she seemed flustered by him. It was weird seeing my mom like that. The Miss Prim and Proper mother of mine became a heated mess. I caught her playing with her chocolate brown hair and giggling like a schoolgirl. After I'd had about enough of it, I told her we had to go.

"You're pretty quiet," Parker states the obvious. I'd become so lost in thought I momentarily forgot where I was. *Parker's car.* Although, I'm not sure where we're going now.

As we pass some houses, I can see the beach in sight. The drive is about thirty minutes from the college.

"Ah, where are we going?" I decide to ignore his statement. Yes, I'd been quiet pondering what he'd said to Devon about talking to me first. I don't think there's much to discuss; we're friends, aren't we? And that's it. Even though I've become a green-eyed monster when he's with another girl, I have no claim over him.

"I'm taking you on the date I won Monday night."

"Umm... were you going to ask first?" I giggle nervously. "I need to get my hand checked, remember?"

Parker's head swings in my direction, taking his focus off the road for a moment. "Is it that bad?" he asks, a softness to his words.

"Yeah, it's quite sore," I say, rubbing my swollen hand gently. I hold it up to him. Something flashes on his face. His lips turn into a thin line of disapproval. Next minute, his car jerks into a turning lane. Once we're sorted and now heading in a different direction he pulls his phone out and quickly types something.

"Where are you going now?" I ask.

"I'm going to take you to the hospital."

"Don't worry. I can go to my doctor."

"No, this will be quicker. My mom is a doctor at the hospital."

Well, there's something I didn't know. I suppose I

don't really know Parker very well. I've never asked him about his family before. I don't even know if he has any siblings. Damn, that's bad. *How could I not have asked sooner?*

We pass by a number of buildings, and then the large white and blue hospital comes into view. I'm actually going to meet his mother. It must be the day for it.

I could honestly say I'd have died of embarrassment thanks to my mother if Parker had seen that little exchange.

Pulling to a stop in the parking lot, Parker's out the door and at mine in seconds.

"Well, aren't you chivalrous?"

"Yep, you know I try my hardest." He has a smoldering look on his face which reminds me of Flynn Rider from *Tangled*.

I shake my head, giving him a grin as I slip from the car. He shuts the door behind me and comes up beside me. I lift my left hand, and he inspects it. His touch leaves a heated prickling sensation over my skin.

"I don't think it's broken—perhaps a sprain. Mom will check it out. I sent her a message to let her know we were coming." Slowly, he puts my hand down and steps around me to my good hand, taking it in his. A flurry of butterflies swarms in my stomach. I'm not sure what's happening between us. But I'm liking it.

"What are you thinking?" Parker asks, the question taking me by surprise.

Do I tell him the truth? Or just act worried about meeting his mom… and my hand, if it's broken?

I remain silent for a moment while I choose. I prefer the truth. I lift our entwined hands.

"I'm wondering what this is?"

Parker's other hand reaches up, rubbing the back of his neck. "What do you want it to be?"

"What do you mean by that? Don't put my own question back on me—I'm asking you. That's what I was thinking about when you asked. Would you have preferred me to not bring it up, and simply go with the flow?" What's going through his mind?

I let him process my words. We hop in the elevator, and he presses the fifth-floor button. I've been in close proximity with him a number of times, only at this moment, there's a sizzling heat sparking between us. If I can feel it, I'm sure he can as well. He grips my hand, his thumb gently rubbing circles on my heated skin. Parker leans right into me. His warm body presses against mine.

"What are you thinking?" I breathe out the same question he asked me moments ago.

"I'm thinking about pushing you against the wall, and devouring those pink lips that taunt me every time I'm around you."

The air in my lungs evaporates. I turn my head to face him. He's so close that his warm breath hits my lips. If I leaned in an inch, our lips would collide. *Is this really happening? Am I dreaming?*

The elevator pings, alerting us we've arrived at our floor.

"Next time I won't hold back." There's promise in his words. We step away from each other, and I catch a glimpse of my pink flushed face in the mirror on the elevator wall. *Why didn't I go in for a kiss?* I want to kick myself.

Parker leads me around the floor. I can tell he knows this place well.

We stop at an office door.

"Hey, Mom," he says casually. Those words increase my heart rate exponentially. I'm not good with the whole meet-the-parents thing. The weird thing is that I met Hayden's parents possibly a handful of times. He wasn't one who liked to be home much. Now, here I am meeting Parker's mom. I'm a bundle of nerves.

"Hey, honey." The woman behind the desk stands and gives Parker a hug. He releases my hand to hug her back.

Parker's mother has sandy blonde hair tied up in a ponytail. She's stunning, and when she comes closer, I see the resemblance between Parker and her. She wears a navy blue business skirt with a buttoned-up white shirt. Her petite build is not where Parker got his solid frame. Her eyes land on me, and she beams a brilliant, white-toothed smile.

"Mom, this is Addison. She hurt her hand today. Addy, this is my mom, Julie."

"Please call me Jules," she corrects Parker, extending her hand to me. I take it with my good one.

"Nice to meet you," I nervously squeak out.

Jules gives me a heartwarming smile. "Let's take a look at your hand."

I raise it for her to inspect.

"How did you do this?" she asks.

I cringe. "Umm… I hit something." I catch a glimpse of Parker, who does nothing to hide his smile. Here I am freaking out that his mom is going to hate me if I say I punched an actual person.

Jules watches me skeptically with raised eyebrows. She flicks her stare at her son. "Hit something?"

Parker bursts into laughter, unable to control himself. "More like someone."

"Parker," I hiss, shocked he's actually told his mother. He says nothing but continues on with his fit of laughter. I look Jules in the eye. "Yes, I hit someone who was harassing my little brother."

"Well, we can't have that now, can we? We best get this x-rayed to check that nothing's broken."

After about an hour, Jules comes back to her office where Parker and I have been waiting in silence.

"It appears, Addison, you have a hairline fracture in your middle metacarpal. With these kinds of fractures you basically only need to rest your hand. Do nothing strenuous and ice it for the next twenty-four to forty-eight hours. Do you have some pain relief at home?"

"Yeah, I think I've got some. I can pop into the store and grab some just in case on the way home," I reply.

"Good idea. Now, this type of injury usually takes around six to eight weeks to heal. How about Parker brings you back for a checkup in about six weeks?" Her smile falls on Parker.

"Subtle, Mom, subtle," he murmurs under his breath while shaking his head. *Did I miss something?*

"I can go see my doctor for the follow up," I say.

Jules smiles. "It's perfectly okay, I'm more than happy to help you." She holds out something for me. I take it, analyzing it.

"It's a wrist brace," she says. "I want you to wear this starting tomorrow. Allow some time for the swelling to go down a little before putting it on."

"Thank you so much for all your help."

She takes a seat behind her desk. "Perhaps next time..." she pauses looking up, ". . . don't hit someone."

I can hear the hidden mirth in her words. It doesn't help that Parker's laughing, yet again, beside me.

"You're a bundle of laughs this afternoon, aren't you?" I shoot the question at him.

Parker holds his hands up in defense. "It's funny. That's all," he says, stifling another laugh. I want to slap him but refrain since his mother's right in front of me.

"Addison, did you want to join us for dinner tonight?"

Parker's chuckles stop immediately. His wide eyes look at me, and he gives me a slight headshake.

Does he want me to say no? Well, I'll screw that plan right up.

"Sure, I'd love to." I give my most pleasant grin to both of them.

Parker shakes his head.

"Great. Paislee would love to meet you."

"Paislee?" I flick the question to Parker, who now has a smug look resting on his face. *Parker and Paislee?* Did their parents plan that?

"Parker's little sister," Julie says.

I guess it's the day to meet each other's family members. Thankfully, Parker got out of meeting my dad.

"Awesome. Sounds good."

Jules stands. "Lovely. Now go, and I'll finish things up here, and see you both at home."

As she completes the sentence, realization dawns on me. I'm going to Parker's house, and not only that, I'm going to be having dinner with his family. What a day it's been.

"Do you want me to pick anything up?" Parker asks as he pecks his mother on the cheek.

"No, I think we have everything for burgers."

We say our goodbyes, and Parker retakes my hand as we move toward the elevator. Once inside, the space becomes smaller than usual when I remember what almost happened last time we were in here and the promise he made.

"So you have a sister, huh?" I quickly throw it out there, not wanting to return to our previous elevator conversation or lack thereof. Not right now anyway.

"Yep. I'm sure she'll love you." He looks down at me, with a mischievous grin on his face.

I suck in a hard breath, and as I do, I inhale his spicy aftershave scent. *How did I miss that smell in the car?* It consumes me, captivates me. Our gazes lock. In one swoop, his lips press against mine, and the wind is knocked from me. I respond to his movement, opening my mouth, and our tongues clash together. Parker comes around in front of me, pressing his heated body against my hungry one—hungry for his hands to claim me.

As quick as his lips were on mine, the elevator pings, alerting us that we've arrived at our floor.

Parker releases me, taking a step back. I lick my lips, wanting to pull him against me again and continue to ride the elevator until we are sated. His hungry stare holds me in place. He lowers his head to my neck.

"I told you I wasn't going to hold back next time," he whispers. Retaking my hand, he leads me to the car. I'm stunned and remain mute.

On the drive to his place, my brain is still unable to process what just happened. *Did it even happen?*

Get a grip, Addison. Yes, it happened. Parker kissed me, and it was so damn good. He held me captive with his lips and tongue, and I wanted more.

I'm still not sure where I stand with him. So much for my vow to keep clear of guys like Hayden. But as my mind thinks of Hayden, I know Parker's nothing like him. Heck, he's happy for me to meet his family, and he treats his mother so well.

Clearing my throat, I say, "So, ah… your sister. What's she like? How old is she?"

I turn to see him snickering. "Really? That's what you want to ask me?"

"No, but—"

"Ask me your question again," Parker cuts in.

"What question?" I ask, puzzled by this game he's playing.

"Think about it. When you figure it out, ask me again."

What question is he referring to? I'm baffled.

When I'm about to question him again, we turn into the driveway of a two-story cream brick home, which stops me. It's not a huge mansion; it appears very homely and welcoming. There's a white Toyota Hatchback in the driveway. The gardens are all perfectly trimmed and the colorful flowers catch my eye. It's breathtaking.

"You have a nice home," I say as I take in all the details.

"Thanks. And it looks like Paislee's here. Brace yourself," he warns.

"Seriously, what's so scary about your sister? It's like you're trying to warn me away from her." I pause and stare at him as he pulls to a stop. "Are you afraid I'll like her more than you?" I waggle my eyebrows at him playfully with a giggle.

He scoffs. "No, I'm more worried that she'll scare you away. She's twenty-one months younger than me, and is a very nosy girl."

"Why isn't she attending college?"

Parker climbs out and comes around to my door, opening it for me once again. "Because she's at boarding school. Let's just say she's a wild one. She'll start freshman year at the college next Monday. She's a little late for intake, but they've allowed it. She just has to catch up on classes." He takes my hand again as I exit the car.

All of a sudden, the question Parker was referring to slaps me in the face. *I asked him what we were.* Deciding now isn't the time to ask it, I leave it on hold for now.

"So you're afraid your sister will corrupt me."

Parker laughs. "Yeah, that's one reason." He opens the front door, yelling, "Pais, I've got someone for you to meet."

A high-pitched scream erupts from the top of the stairs, and it scares me. Parker gives me a sideways glance and an 'Are you ready for this?' face. Now, I'm not so sure.

Loud and fast footsteps run through the hall until a long-haired beauty stands at the top step, staring down at us. Then she screams again. *Is this girl crazy?*

She bounds down the stairs two at a time. Yep, I'm a little worried now. She pulls up in front of me. Her eyes follow the length of my body. Now that's something I would expect from her brother. I look to Parker wide-eyed, asking him the silent question: *What's her deal?*

He shrugs. The smile on his face tells me he's not going to help me.

"Oh, I know I'm going to like her, Parker. Hi, I'm Paislee." Instead of a typical handshake or awkward hello wave-type thing, Paislee wraps her arms around me, pulling me in for a hug. She smells like apple spray or body wash. It's weird; I can't wrap my arms around her since her hug's somehow blocked my arms at my sides.

"Ease up, Pais. She has a sore hand," Parker tells his sister.

Paislee releases me right away.

"Pais, this is Addison."

Paislee's smile is the same as Parker and his mother's. She has long sandy blonde hair, and the exact same eyes. Gee, can't half tell they're siblings. Paislee is a stunner, and I'm sure she's going to have the guys flocking to her at college.

"Nice to meet you. What happened to your hand?" She spots my swollen hand, and her brow furrows.

Parker answers before I can, "She hit someone."

Paislee's mouth drops. "Really?" she squeals.

Oh, my goodness, she's going to crack the windows if she keeps that up. I want to block my ears the noise is so high.

"Yep. Some dick was harassing her brother, so she took care of it. Of course, we were there to back her up," he says, sounding proud of himself.

"Perhaps if one of you guys had hit him before he shot his mouth off, I wouldn't have a sore hand," I retort.

Paislee claps excitedly. "Oh, yeah, I'm going to like her," she says, then turns to her brother. "Why didn't you drop the guy instead of her? Some hero you are."

It's my turn to laugh. "I think I'm going to like you too, Paislee," I say.

Parker shakes his head. "Someone save me."

CHAPTER
Seventeen

ules arrives home not long after Parker and me. The house is alive with buzz and chatter. While Paislee and Jules prepare dinner, Parker shows me around their home. When you come through the door to the left, there's a living room, and on the right's an office. The kitchen and dining rooms are behind the living room.

Parker takes my hand and leads me up the stairs. To the left is his mom and dad's room, although there's been no mention of his father for some reason. Up the other end of the hallway are Paislee and Parker's rooms. They share a bathroom also. A perfect home in all ways.

"Nice place," I say as he pulls me into his room.

Given he lives somewhere else right now, I didn't expect there to be too much here. He has a queen-sized bed, a desk, a television, and stereo system set up. "Why don't you live here while going to school, wouldn't it save you some money?"

Parker scrunches up his face. "Nah, I like to have privacy from my mother and sister. They're nosy girls." He chuckles while dropping onto the couch in front of his bed. "Paislee's going to be all up in your business when she comes to school. She may be a freshman, but she'll act like a junior and try to run the school."

She sounds overly confident. I move across and sit with him. "I like her already."

"Figured you might." He takes my good arm and pulls me against him. I rest against him, my sore hand lying on his chest. I mold into his side while his finger gently traces over my puffed up hand.

"I'm sorry," he says, shocking me.

Twisting my head, I look up at him. His focus remains on my fingers. "What are you sorry for?" I ask, puzzled.

Parker shuts his eyes for a moment. "I should have been the one who hit that guy. Not you. Then this wouldn't have happened."

His affection makes my heart want to burst.

"Hey?" I ask. Parker opens his eyes and searches mine. "It's not your fault. I wasn't focused on my punch. It's my own decision. When it comes to Devon, everything's different. He's my brother, and people look at him and treat him differently. It infuriates me when people like that dick-bag mistreat him. I lost my cool. Now, I need to suffer the consequences." Even the mention of the dick-bag gets my blood boiling.

Parker's arms tighten around me. "You're a feisty one, little mouse." He grins down at me. There's hunger in his gaze. My stomach tightens. I'm 100 percent sure he can feel the vibrations of my heart against his chest.

"Only when I have to be," I breathe.

Parker draws his lip between his teeth, pressing his forehead against mine. "Little mouse, you do something to me. You taste like sweet candy, and after that sample in the elevator, I want more." His voice is deep and wanting.

Without hesitation, I push myself up. Our lips connect. His hand reaches up, pulling my hair-tie from my ponytail. My long hair falls around my face, and Parker's hand dives in. He entwines his fingers through it, pressing me against his hungry mouth. Our tongues dance together in harmony.

In one swoop, Parker lifts me into his lap so I'm straddling him. We continue devouring each other. His warm hands find my bare skin under my T-shirt. A groan escapes me while his hand massages my skin.

There's a loud rap at the door. I leap off him, paranoid his mother is about to walk in on us getting busy.

"Dinner's ready," Paislee's chirpy voice sounds behind the door. I breathe a sigh of relief, and Parker starts chuckling beside me.

"I don't think I've had someone get off me that quick, little mouse."

"I didn't want your mother walking in on me dry-humping you in her house," I squeak.

Parker takes my arm, gently pulling me back to him. "You make me laugh." He gives me one last kiss before standing, and I follow him out of the room.

It's dark when we leave Parker's house about two hours later. I think Parker had had enough of Paislee giving him googly eyes. She doesn't seem like one to hold back, and she more than showed it by asking me twenty questions. I think Parker learned more about me during her interrogation than he has at any other time.

Once we escaped and were in the car, Parker heaved a sigh of relief. Jules helped me get the wrist brace on and showed me how I should adjust it as the swelling goes down.

As we drive back to the school, I have a question which has been burning inside me. I need to know the answer. "Can I ask you something?"

Parker nods. "Shoot."

"Where's your dad?" I watch Parker, and take note of his reaction. His grip on the steering wheel tightens, and his head twitches slightly. "If you don't want to talk about it that's all right," I quickly add.

Parker rubs his face. "We don't discuss Dad much. He left when Paislee was only a few months old. I don't remember much about him, to be honest. It's always just been the three of us. Mom got herself through school to become a doctor, and we went without a lot of things growing up. My mom is truly an inspiration."

Don't I feel like a complete idiot now? "Oh. I'm so sorry for asking."

Parker shrugs. "It is what it is." The sadness in his tone slams me in the stomach. I reach across to him, placing my hand on his leg. He gently rests his hand on mine, since it's my strapped one. "Don't feel bad. I knew you'd ask. Everyone does at some point."

I rub my thumb over his jeans. "Still, it must be hard answering when you don't know much about your dad."

I can't imagine my life without my father. Yes, he's a workaholic, but I know if I need him for anything he'll be there no matter what.

"It is hard, but Mom's never kept anything from us. If either Paislee or I want to know or meet our father, she's said she won't stop us. Over time, I think she's stopped hating him. As you can see, she's done an amazing job all on her own."

"She really is nothing short of amazing."

Silence fills the cabin of the car. It's not uncomfortable—it feels more like there's a lot we're both thinking about.

I watch as we pass the cars and the beach. It's dark. The glow of the moon lights up the ocean, and the waves crashing as they hit the shore. We head toward the hill. At the top is a statue in the shape of a boat. It's called The Singing Ship. When the wind blows on the pipes they have attached to it, it sounds like a soft hum. It's peaceful, although I've never actually been here at nighttime.

"Still taking me on that date, huh?" I ask as we pull to a stop.

Parker turns to me. "I won it fair and square, so now I can enjoy it."

The cheekiness in his smile makes me laugh. He climbs out of the car and comes around to open my door. As I step out into the night air, the salty ocean smell is all around me. I love the beach. It's a thought-provoking place. Simply walking along the shore sends my mind into overdrive and puts my worries at ease.

Parker throws his arm around my shoulders, pulling me into him tightly. He leads me to a bench to the left of The Singing Ship. I can hear the light hum. It's as though it sings with the song of my heart. A sense of peace wraps around me. I don't care what's happened during these last few weeks. What counts is now. Right here in this moment, I know I should be with Parker. As much as I didn't want this to happen, it's happening, and I'm falling. I only hope Parker will catch me if I stumble.

He takes a seat and pulls me firmly against him. It's a coolish night. We sit and listen to the waves crashing against the shore. I let my head fall on Parker's shoulder. His hand comes up and starts running through my hair.

"Can I ask you something?" he questions, the husk to his voice sending a shiver down my spine.

"If you keep playing with my hair like that, you can ask me anything," I moan a little too loudly.

His soft chuckle vibrates through me. "All right… tell me what the deal is with you and your sister."

I groan. "Really? You want to know?"

"I asked the question."

"I'm honestly not sure why she hates Devon and me so much. There was a time when we were younger, and we were the best of friends. Then, as the years went on, she grew up, got bitchy friends, and in turn began treating me like the dirt she walked on."

Parker releases a whistle. "So there's no real reason."

I shrug. "I'm not sure what the problem is. Then when I started coming to college and she was in her sorority, I think she was worried I'd try and pledge with her. That stuff doesn't interest me. I want to become a teacher to help kids with special needs… kids like Devon." A lump catches in my throat, thinking of the others out there who need that little extra help that Devon receives.

Parker places his finger under my chin, tilting my head so I look him in the eyes. The image of the moon glows in his eyes. My heart beats furiously. Our gazes stay locked on each other. "You're something else, Addison," he pauses, before continuing. "I have another question."

I don't risk speaking but merely nod.

"Would you ever go back to Hayden?"

I jerk out of his arms and stare at him with disgust. "Do you really think I would?"

"I'm just asking." His voice is slightly raised, and his arms are held up in defense.

"I don't think I could ever go back to him." I hang my head and stare down at my hands sitting in my lap. "He isn't someone who's healthy for anyone to be in a relationship with, if that even makes sense."

Parker's hand clenches and releases. "Do you know why I gave you that note? The first one?"

I shake my head. "Where are you going with this?"

"I wanted you to know you could call me if you ever needed help. I saw how he looked at you that day when you pulled away from him." Parker pulls me back to him. I can't take my eyes from his. I have this feeling he's going to say more. My stomach is doing flips like a trapeze artist. Parker puffs out a breath and continues, "I'll be honest, Addison. I was scared for you."

"You and me both," I respond.

"It took everything in me not to lash out at him then and there. When I saw the fear in your eyes, I knew I needed to try and be someone you could trust and rely on. Yes, I can be a jerk, but I would never treat someone how he treated you. I'd watched from afar long enough to know how much you'd lost your sparkle."

I shake my head at all the words Parker says. "I'm sorry, what?"

"Since I laid eyes on you last year I've wanted you. When you were with Hayden, I always wanted you to be with me. That night at the party, I put myself in your path so often that you couldn't resist me." He chuckles, shaking his head. I sit in stunned silence as he puts everything out in the open. "After I kissed you, it only made me want you even more, and then you went back to that douchebag. It all backfired on me. After that night, I saw you change. The happiness you had was gone— diminished. Now I know I sound like a crazy stalker person."

I'm sure I need to collect my mouth off the bench and shut it. All my walls and worries crumble away. Parker has dug deep into my soul.

After a moment, Parker cups my cheek. "Say something," he whispers.

What am I meant to say after something so earth-shattering? Never have I ever had someone analyze me like Parker has. "Why didn't you just tell me that night at the party, or even after that?" *Why didn't he?*

"I went to, but I'd caught you begging Hayden for forgiveness after what you'd done. I felt that no matter what I said you'd think I was some basketball jock searching for his next friends with benefits."

"Yeah, that's probably what I would have thought." I throw it out there playfully, shoving his shoulder. His warm lips press against my temple. Lifting my head, I glance up at him, then press my mouth to his. This kiss feels different from the others. They were lustful and desire-filled; this one is slow, sensual, meaningful, and claiming. He can have my heart, but if he breaks it, I'm not sure I'll recover from the hurt.

Pulling back, I say, "So I have a question for you now."

Parker's mouth presses against my neck, and I moan with excitement. "Shoot." His breath tickles my neck, so I push him back to see his face.

"So what is this?" My hand gestures between us.

"I want you to be mine, Addison." Parker holds my gaze.

I want to throw myself at him, but keep my composure somehow. "Then I'm all yours, Parker."

CHAPTER
Eighteen

"Are you freakin' serious?" Elsie screams at me loud enough that I have to block my ears. I watch her jump around our bedroom excitedly. I came back to our dorm quiet as a mouse, only once I lightly clicked the bedroom door closed, Elsie sprang out of bed and demanded to know where I'd been and what was happening. So I told her everything. My cheeks hurt because I couldn't wipe the smile off my face as I let her know every single detail of the afternoon and night.

Elsie squeals excitedly. "Be quiet, Elsie. I don't want another family meeting at a stupid hour." I love the other girls, but I'm wanting to see if Parker lets his friends know about our relationship before I go blurting things out and sounding like an idiot if something backfires on me.

Elsie stops in front of me, taking hold of my shoulders. Her eyes are wide with excitement. "I'm sorry, I'm so happy right now. I told you to go for him." She shakes me slightly, and I shrug out of her grip and stand from my bed.

"I'm still scared," I admit honestly.

She stops. A soft, knowing smile sits on her face. "I know. It'll be all right. Parker's different. I'm sure you must see that."

"Oh, I do. I still can't help thinking that something's going to ruin it, and in turn, ruin me all over again."

Elsie sits down on her bed, and I fall back onto mine. We face each other. Elsie's a friend who'll always give it to me straight. She'll tell me if I need deodorant—that's how blunt she can be.

"You were hurt last time. Your boyfriend was a controlling freak, and you're so much better off without him. Parker's different. He may seem like a player, but keep in mind now you've met his mom and sister. Is his relationship with them good?"

I nod, listening intently to where she's going with this. I already feel a small amount of my apprehension about the whole thing lifting.

Elsie continues, "If a guy treats his family great, even his little sister, then he's a good one. Have fun with this, Addison. This *is* a good thing."

I know she's right. I need to let it play out, no matter the outcome. "All right and if this all falls apart, you better be there to pick up the pieces."

"You know I'm always here for you." She leaps toward me, giving me a hug. "I'm so excited for you," she whispers excitedly in my ear.

I laugh. I'm excited as well. Never did I think Parker would go for me. Everything he admitted to me tonight shocked me. If he'd have told me how he felt earlier, I probably would have ended things a long time ago with Hayden. Instead, I stuck around hoping things would get better.

I was wrong.

Elsie and I take a seat at an outside table, since we both have a free hour. The sun's shining, and the breeze is refreshing. Elsie's still gushing over the whole Parker thing. I haven't seen or heard from him today. It makes me a little nervous. He did say last night that he had early morning practice, so I'll put it down to that.

"Any word from Parker?" Elsie asks, as if she can read my thoughts.

I twist the lid off my soda. "Nope. He said he had an early practice. I've still not heard anything." I take a mouthful of my salad and then look out over the rest of campus. College is always so busy. It's also party central. Every day there's a new break-up or some story of who hooked up with who over the weekend. *I wonder what will be said about me?*

There was lots said when everything happened with Hayden. Now there's something new for everyone to talk about.

"Oh, I'm sure he'll show up," Elsie says.

I know he will. It still doesn't stop my mind running through a million different scenarios until he does. What if Stacey's cornered him and has managed to get in his pants again? Or even… my sister? And let's not forget about *Barbie*.

All three are possibilities.

I don't think Parker would do that, though. I hate my stupid overthinking brain sometimes.

"What are our plans this weekend? Did you know it's the first basketball game this Friday?" Elsie asks.

"Parker told me about it last night. He asked me to go. I said I'd see."

Elsie's eyes widen in shock. "Why did you say that? You're together now, aren't you? So why are you saying something like... *you'll see?*"

"I know, Elsie." I sigh. "I need to see if things are different first. He can sit there and say, yes we're together, but it means nothing to me unless he shows me. For example, messaging me, showing up, and planting a kiss on me in public, or something similar."

Elsie sits across from me with her arms folded across her chest. I can tell she's annoyed at my response. "Don't give me that stupid talk, Addison. It's time to stop thinking he's anything like Hayden. Hayden was, and still is, a dick. We both know this, and I already see a difference with Parker. When you mention his name, you smile." She's grinning at me, and I do the same. Especially when she mentions Parker. My stomach does a million flips at the mention of his name.

"I know. I know."

Elsie's face turns to stone before me. Turning in my seat, I see what's gotten her into bitch mode. Stacey stands behind me.

I get up from my seat, not giving her the satisfaction of me looking up at her. "Can I help you?" I ask as politely as possible.

Stacey is flanked by her flock of ass-kissers. She's wearing a tight shirt with a bright pink bra underneath, leaving nothing to people's imaginations. Throw in her Daisy Duke cutoffs, and she's asking for every person to check out her butt cheeks.

Stacey gives me a once-over before meeting my eyes. "I thought I told you to stay away from Parker."

And here it goes. I fold my arms across my chest. "Whatever happens between Parker and me is none of your concern," I state, matter-of-factly. The smile falls from her face and a blaze lights in her eyes. She takes a step closer. I don't budge, not letting her get to me. She's pathetic and needs to grow up.

"Oh, that's where you're wrong. You see, he was with me this morning, if you know what I mean."

My composure falters slightly. I try to pull myself back together, only she's caught my slip. An evil smile twists on her lips, and her pearly whites shine at me.

Clearing my throat, I say, "I find it hard to believe."

I know he had practice. There'd be no reason for him to see her.

Stacey shrugs. "Why not ask him yourself?"

Her focus is on something behind me. I don't need to turn around to know it's Parker. My body hums in his presence. He comes to stand beside me. He doesn't touch me or wrap his arms around me like I thought he would. Now that's what a boyfriend should do to ward off the predators like Stacey.

He does nothing.

He doesn't offer a single touch!

"Hey Parker," Stacey says in her little posh, snooty, pathetic voice, shuffling a little closer to him. "It was good *catching up* this morning." She winks at him.

It's taking everything I have to not lose it at the both of them. I can feel small parts of me crumbling. I won't give Stacey the satisfaction of seeing me lose it, though.

Parker stands there. I can't bring myself to look up at

him. If I do, I know it'll break me. I'm waiting desperately for him to shut down what she's saying, and for him to plant a kiss on my lips to prove to her that we're together now and she has no chance.

The silence he responds with is deafening.

Turning my head, I glance up at his troubled features, and his worried eyes catch mine. In that moment, I know Stacey's speaking the truth.

A day.

Our relationship didn't even last a single twenty-four hours.

How pathetic.

Don't I feel like the fool, once again?

Parker finally opens his mouth to speak. I hold my breath.

Stacey jumps in. "Look at this photo of us."

Parker looks between her and I. His brow furrows. She holds out her phone to me, and my resolve crumbles. There's a picture of Parker and Stacey locking lips.

"Don't listen to her, Addison. It's an old photo."

I don't want to hear any more. I lift my bag and run. Elsie hurries after me. I hear Parker's raised voice, but I can't make out what he's saying. I take off so fast that I lose Elsie for a moment.

I keep running until I'm back at the dorm, and shut away in my room. I quickly close down my cell, not wanting to see what Parker has to say. He should have made a statement by kissing me or holding me so Stacey could see that he was with me, yet he stood there in silence when she mentioned the *catch-up* this morning.

A puffed Elsie pushes open the door. "Stop!" She takes a huge gulp of air before continuing, "Don't think the worst. Did you hear what he said to her as you were taking a jog?"

"Why the hell should I listen to him? I knew this was a bad idea from the start, and I let my silly feelings take over. I should have kept my vow to myself to not date guys like Parker or Hayden." I scream into my pillow for a second before it's yanked away from me.

"Will you shut up a moment?" Elsie yells at me. It's like a verbal slap across the face. She's never spoken to me like that.

"What?" I yell back, equally annoyed.

"He told her to leave him alone. That he's with you now, and there's no chance of him and her getting back together."

Elsie's words slowly sink in.

"Then why the hell didn't he say that when I was standing right there?" I shout, my frustrations and anger getting the better of me.

Is that because I know Stacey was only trying to get under my skin?

And I let her. I'm so angry at myself.

"Perhaps they did catch up this morning. You know Stacey—she's a manipulator, and she knew you and Parker had become close. She did this to get you not to trust him so she could keep trying. And it damn well worked." Elsie releases a puff of air. "Stop thinking the worst."

"I'm trying," I yell back.

"Is everything okay in here?" Willow asks hesitantly as she pokes her head into the room.

"Yes," Elsie and I yell in unison.

Willow quickly slinks back out the door.

A tense silence fills our bedroom as I collapse onto my bed.

"I'm sorry," I say after a moment.

"Me too," Elsie says as she comes and sits beside me.

"I let Stacey get under my skin, and come between Parker and me."

"You did. Now you've realized this, you need to go and fix it."

Rising from my bed, I grab my bag, ready to find Parker. I pull the door open, stopping in my tracks. There he stands with Willow.

CHAPTER
Nineteen

"Well, well... look who it is," Elsie says, nudging me. She has on her I-told-you-so face. I roll my eyes at her.

"Ah... did you hear that?" I ask nervously.

Parker chuckles, a playfulness in his stare. "Only a small part," he replies holding up his finger and thumb showing me just how much. Parker turns to Elsie. "Thanks for sticking up for me."

"Don't go screwing it up, because if you do hurt her, I'll castrate you."

His hand drops. He grips his crotch, a worried expression on his face.

I burst out laughing. "Stop it, Elsie. It'll be both of us doing it."

A horrified look replaces the worried one on Parker's face. "Come on, girls," Parker groans. "You're killing me here."

We laugh, and Willow joins in.

"Come on, Willow. Let's leave these two to talk," Elsie says as she grabs her bag from the table and walks out the door, but Willow stares between the two of us.

"You need to fill me in, girl," Willow states, pointing her finger at me.

"You know I will," I promise.

Once they leave, Parker steps closer to me. My body ignites at his proximity. He cups my cheek. "I'm sorry," he says. "I should have handled the situation better. Instead, I became so worried what you'd think if you found out that she came to see me. She's been trying to get me back since I caught her with Hayden. You're not really going to castrate me, are you?" He almost sounds nervous.

I giggle. "If you keep it in your pants then your bits will survive." I pause for a moment, gathering my thoughts before continuing, "I'm sorry as well. I overreacted and thought the worst of you. I should have known she'd do something like this."

Parker pulls me against his firm chest, his spicy scent wrapping around my senses and drawing me in. His hand grips the back of my neck. It's like he's massaging the desire within me, willing it to come out and play.

"You need to know. Yes, she came to see me. I told her I was with you now, and that she needed to leave me alone. She obviously took that as an invitation to try getting between us. I honestly thought it had worked."

I glance up at him, and there's a torn expression on his face.

"I feel like I've waited forever to have you, and now I've got you I don't want to lose you," he whispers, burying his face into my neck, causing goose bumps over my skin. My chest tightens with affection and want.

"I guess I have some insecurities to get over. You'll have to put up with my mood swings," I breathe. The way his hands trace over me makes me short of breath.

Parker peppers feather-light kisses along my neck before claiming my lips. He drives his tongue into my mouth. He tastes sweet.

"I'll put up with anything when it comes to you, little mouse." His breath tickles my lips. "I'm going to claim you as mine, and then everyone will know. You wait." He sounds like a caveman, claiming what's his. He can have me. My body tingles all over, thriving off every single breath and touch between us. He sets my soul on fire and I crave every part of him.

Parker's fingers grip the bottom of my shirt, and then he lifts it over my head in one swift move.

"Bedroom," I whisper as his pecks leave their warmth along my collarbone.

Lifting me up, he takes me to the bedroom. I gesture to my bed. He kicks the door shut behind us and places me gently down on the mattress. His large frame hovers over the top of me. He dives in kissing me like he couldn't breathe without me. I find the bottom of his shirt, pulling it off. Of course, he has to help me a little, since I'm slightly immobile with one of my hands.

Parker grinds himself against me, his bare chest brushing my breasts. I groan, throwing my head back as he devours my neck and nips his way toward my breasts. He unclasps my black lace bra, tossing it aside. Both his hands grip my breasts, and he slowly massages them, arousing me more, before his mouth gets busy with them.

"You taste so good," he moans.

His skin against mine is smooth to the touch. I crave him. I want every part of him. I've never wanted something as badly as I want Parker Kent to claim my soul. He reaches down, undoing my jeans. Leaning back on his heels, he pulls them off and makes quick work of his own.

He stands before me. I'm left dumbfounded by his god-like body.

Slowly, he climbs over me. My fingertips glide over every inch of his body. Goose bumps rise on his olive skin.

Our bodies soon become one entangled mess. His hand glides over my tenderness; his mouth swallows my moans. He makes me feel everything, every single emotion describable.

"Oh, little mouse, I should have tried harder for you a year ago. You're something special." He pecks a few more kisses on my lips and neck. "You've well and truly stolen my heart."

"How was the make-up session?" Elsie asks as she walks in the door a few hours later. I'm planted on the couch in the main room of our dorm. Obviously, I didn't make it to the remainder of my classes for the day. Parker left about twenty minutes ago since he has another practice session. He made me promise to come to his game on Friday, and of course, I said yes. How could I not after that? "Well?" Elsie prompts.

I'm sure my smile is blinding. "Yeah, good." I sigh happily.

"That good, huh?" She drops down beside me. "There's already rumors traveling around about you and Parker."

"I don't care. I'm done caring."

Elsie's eyebrows shoot up. "This is a side of you I like: relaxed and sated." She giggles.

I shove her in the arm playfully. "Shut up."

"Now really, how was he? I need some sort of details. I'm living vicariously through you right now."

I laugh. I'm sure she's been sated at the recent parties we've been to, but she only tells me about the memorable one-night stands.

"He was *good*," I assure her.

"How good?"

"Think of your most favorite thing and times it by…" I pause, thinking. "Heck… I can't even give you a number. Let's say ten times better than Hayden. The way he caressed a *certain* part of my body." I repress a groan. "I would have happily been locked in our room for a lot longer."

Elsie screws her face up. "Eww… so our room smells like sex now." I laugh. "Shut up! That's nasty! I don't want to *smell* everything."

Tears fall down my face, and my chest hurts from laughing too much. "Oh, you're killing me, Elsie. Don't worry. It won't smell of sex." I can't contain myself.

"It better not, or there'll be problems between us. It's like you're taunting me—that you're getting good sex and I'm getting like *nothing*."

"Oh, my goodness." I fall to the floor, rolling around. Laughter fills the room. Elsie scowls at me from the couch. I can see she's playing with me. I know she's happy for me. She's my best friend; she can't stay mad forever.

After a moment of watching me writhing in fits of laughter at her expense, she says, "You better go spray that room with something. I don't want anything assaulting my nostrils unless it smells pretty, or it's me that's made the room smell of sex."

Slowly, I pull myself from the floor and go spray some body perfume around the room and over my bed, shaking my head as I do. Walking back to the couch, I tease, "The coast is clear."

"I still love you," she says, disappearing into the bedroom. "What the hell happened in here?"

I erupt again, knowing that would be her response. Standing, I glide into the bedroom.

"I don't know what you mean. Isn't the room always this messy?"

My clothes are scattered around the room from where they landed when Parker stripped me; some are even on her bed. Parker's shirt also lays across her belongings.

"Don't act so innocent. You're not my friend anymore," she shouts. "Did he leave half-naked or something?"

I giggle. "No, he put on a spare shirt he had in his bag and left that one here. I'll be claiming that now."

She throws all of my stuff over on my bed, huffing as she does it. "We'll need some ground rules if this is going to be a regular occurrence. I'm happy for you, though." She loves me too much to be annoyed at me.

"Sure, ground rules." I nod, still grinning.

"Even as you sit there I can tell by the little glint in your eyes that you have no intention of following rules."

I shrug.

Elsie walks away shaking her head. "You owe me dinner tonight as payment for using the room for sex."

I pick up Parker's shirt and bring it to my nose. Inhaling his scent sends a quiver shooting through my stomach.

I can't wait to see him again.

CHAPTER
Twenty

I sit with Elsie, Willow, and Jane as we watch everyone pile into the basketball stadium. It's the first game of the season, and electricity is in the air. Stacey and her cheerleading squad are doing their dance on the court. There's a lot of cheering and excitement. From the corner of my vision, I spot someone waving. It's Paislee. I smile and give her a wave back.

"Who are you waving at?" Elsie asks, her voice raised to speak over the noise.

"Parker's sister. It looks like she's coming toward us."

Paislee makes her way through the crowd to our seats. "Hey," she squeals, giving me a hug.

"Hey! How are you?" I ask.

"Yeah, I'm enjoying doing nothing at home. Although, I think Mom isn't happy about it."

We laugh together.

"Oh, sorry, these are my friends Elsie, Willow, and Jane." All the girls wave and give a hello. "Girls, this is Paislee. Parker's sister."

Their mouths form perfect Os as they most likely see the resemblance to her brother.

"She'll be going here hopefully next week as a freshman," I say.

Suddenly, loud cheering erupts around us. I turn my focus to the court as I spot the trio coming on with their fellow teammates.

We all cheer and clap. Paislee and Elsie whistle. My eyes are glued to the number-two jersey. The boys begin warming up. Parker scans the stands, stopping when he spots me. I'm sure nothing can wipe away the silly grin plastered across my face.

He graces me with one of his heart-melting smiles. He presses his index and middle finger to his lips, then sends the kiss my way with a wink. My stomach flutters and some of the faces in the crowd turn my way—mostly girls.'

"Oh my goodness, my brother is smooching all over you," Paislee says excitedly. "Did you see the girls giving you dirty looks just now?"

"I don't really care. They can hate me, but I have the guy." I give her a cheeky wink.

"I love you." She bounces excitedly, gripping my good arm. Thankfully.

The whistle blows, and the guys on the court get moving. I trace every movement Parker makes. He's so fluid, his every move precise and flawless. Jimmy and Dane are always close at hand, as are the other players.

I hold my breath as Parker drives the ball down the court. He hits the three-pointer line and takes a shot. As the ball leaves his hands, a player from the other team slams him in the side. My hands fly to my mouth. A series of boos fills the stadium. Parker falls to the ground. He doesn't move for a moment. Dane and Jimmy are by his side immediately. I shoot to my feet, my fingers in my mouth as I chew on my nails waiting for Parker to make some movement.

"What's going on?" I ask the girls around me, hoping they can give me something. My question is pointless, but I still ask it.

"It's all right; he's been hit like this before. He's probably winded. Don't stress." Paislee's assurance is only a small comfort. Of course, she's watched her brother a number of times. My brain continues to try and assure my racing heart.

The coach calls for a time-out. As he gets to Parker, Parker sits and gives a thumbs-up. Cheers and clapping surround us. I release the breath I've been holding. Oh, thank goodness. He jumps to his feet, and his eyes meet mine. Again, he kisses those two fingers and sends them my way followed by a wink.

I'm not cut out to watch these games. I'm always worried someone I care about will get hurt. I've heard stories where people injure themselves so severely that they can't play again. I'd hate for that to happen to Parker. He'd be devastated. I can see the passion he has for the game.

We're finally at the last five minutes of the game. I swear I've held my breath so many times tonight, and cheered the loudest when our team got the ball in. The girls are equally as loud.

Elsie leans over. "It's nice to see you finally enjoying yourself at a game instead of either not going, or just sitting and wallowing like you would do at Hayden's football games."

That statement's true. I hated going to his games. Not once did I feel welcome.

"This, being with Parker—it feels different."

"I know. I can see how happy you've been," Elsie says.

The whistle blows, drawing my attention back to the game. I look at the scoreboard. It's a tie, with one minute left on the clock. Seriously! This kind of thing happens in the NBA so much. It's nail-biting stuff. I love close games like this.

"Come on, River Valley," Elsie and Paislee shout in unison.

After the teams speak to their coaches, they take their spots across the court. Parker glances in my direction, a devious crooked grin on his face. My heart rate spikes.

"Go River Valley," I shout, my voice followed by a number of loud cheers.

Everything around me fades away as the referee blows his whistle again, and then Parker has the ball passed to him from Dane. He drives the ball down the court, and slam dunks a shot. The other team quickly take their pass from the end of the court. They make their way to their hoop, taking a three-pointer shot, only to miss.

My heart sits in my throat as I watch the final minutes of the game. Elsie bounces in her seat, while Willow and Jane watch. Paislee is out of her seat, jumping up and down.

Jimmy catches the rebound and passes it to Parker who passes to Dane, who's farther up the court. Dane takes it the whole way, and I look at the clock—there are ten seconds remaining.

I hear Parker shout, "Shoot it!"

Dane stops at the three-pointer line and takes the shot. I chew on my lip, holding my breath. Time slows down as the ball flies through the air and slowly sinks through the hoop.

I'm on my feet, cheering, as is the rest of the arena.

"Hell, yeah!" Paislee shouts. "Go, boys!"

The team all slap each other on their backs and give manly embraces. Parker turns my way. My smile is so huge that my cheeks hurt. Parker sprints off the court and comes up through the seats. People give him high-fives and slaps on the back, but his eyes remain focused on me.

"What's he doing?" Elsie asks, and I shrug.

Parker makes his way to our row and comes toward me. Paislee stands on her seat, allowing him the space.

In one swift move, his arms slide around my waist, his fingers gripping my hips and his lips brush against mine. The air in my lungs whooshes out. I press myself against his body as we drink in the moment.

He pulls back, hunger burning in his eyes. I desperately didn't want the kiss to end.

"Now they *all* know you belong to me," he says.

I beam at him, throwing my arms around his neck and kissing him passionately once more.

We leave the arena with Paislee tagging along with us. She and Willow are hitting it off.

"Are you girls going to the party tonight?" Paislee asks as we walk back to our dorm.

"Which one?" Elsie asks. She's the one who knows the details about each and every party going on around campus.

"The one at the basketball team house? Like, come on… you're dating the captain of the team. You have to make an appearance." Paislee gestures to me.

Going to a party hadn't even crossed my mind. I have work tomorrow, but the thought of seeing Parker again makes my insides turn to mush.

"Yeah, I'll go," I say.

The girls all cheer.

"Let's get wasted," Elsie says excitedly.

In theory, it's a good idea, yet after my last encounter with alcohol, the aftermath wasn't so good.

"How about you all can get wasted, and I'll watch." I laugh.

"No!" all four of them shout at me.

I turn to Paislee. "How would Parker feel about seeing you drunk?" I ask.

Paislee shrugs. "It's not like he hasn't seen me in that state before."

"Well, if he does say anything, I'll direct his anger toward you," I state.

"He doesn't stay mad at me long for anything. I'm his little sister, but he looks out for me and doesn't stay uptight for longer than a day."

"It's not you I'm worried he'll ignore."

"It'll be all right. Let's have some fun, girls," she shouts.

We arrive at our floor in our building and open the door to our room.

After shutting the door, Elsie yells, "Let's get drunk, girls!" She scurries off, pulling bottles of tequila and Midori from her special stash. "Pineapple juice's in the fridge," she says to Jane, who races off to go grab it.

Jane returns with shot glasses and plastic cups and the juice. "Oh, what the heck? Give me a shot and a Midori Illusion."

Midori and pineapple juice is the nicest drink. It's so sweet. I won't be mixing the hard drinks tonight; I have no reason to. Hayden can do and say whatever he wants, and if that's dating my sister, then so be it. I honestly don't care anymore.

Two hours after getting back to our dorm, we finally leave for the party. Parker's been messaging me asking when I am coming. Every time I've told him I was waiting for the girls. It was partly true. I wanted to look smoking for him. All the girls have had their say and opinion on what I should wear, and not wear. In the end, I settled for black tights with a loose-fitting pale pink button-up top. It's not what Elsie would class as sexy, but I'm comfortable and being true to myself.

We arrive at the party, and it's in full swing. Music vibrates off the walls, and people are making out in the corners. Paislee spots some of her friends and goes over to greet them. I scan the room, looking for any sign of Parker. I catch sight of Dane and make my way to him instead.

I tap his shoulder. He turns, giving me a grin. "Hey," he shouts. "Parker's out back." He throws his thumb over his shoulder, pointing toward the back door.

"Thanks," I yell, and make my way out back. The girls follow me outside.

"There he is, over near the fence with someone,"

Willow says, pointing to a darkened corner. *Why would he be hiding out there?*

My chest begins to ache. This better not turn into something like what happened with Hayden.

I make my way toward Parker. Elsie, Willow, and Jane are in tow. I hear Elsie bristling as she mutters curses under her breath.

As I get closer, I recognize who's with Parker. *Can't my sister keep her claws off my guys?*

Elsie grabs my arm, but I shove her off and surge toward Parker and Ella.

CHAPTER
Twenty One

I stop short. Parker's eyes meet mine. They're soft and warm, but I don't care. This doesn't feel right.

"What's the deal, Ella? You can't find a man of your own, so you have to take mine instead?" I ask. Pure venom drips from my words. So much hate pulses through my veins. I can't help it.

Slowly, she turns to face me. Not a single emotion registers on her face. She actually looks sad. It's not a look she wears often.

Parker steps closer to me. "It's not what you think, Addison."

I laugh. "Oh, yeah, and she doesn't have a hidden agenda to get in your pants."

"Look, I'll just go. Can you deal with *this?*" Ella asks.

Parker gives her a nod, and she leaves Parker, myself, and

the girls gawking after her. *What the heck? She's not being a bitch like she usually is to me.*

I turn to Parker. "You better not be playing up on me." I jab him in the chest with my finger. He takes my hand in his, and I start to feel the fires within me simmer. How am I ever going to stay mad at him if he has this effect on me? I'll never win against him.

"Little mouse, you really think I'm like that lowlife?" He reaches up, tucking some loose hair behind my ear, and rests his hand against my cheek. Then he gives me a smoldering look.

Oh, gosh, I'm done for.

"Well, hell, how can anyone win against those smooth moves?" Elsie pipes up, saying almost what I was thinking. She's spot on. No wonder girls attach themselves to Parker. He's too sweet.

"We'll leave you two be to sort this out, and if you leave, message me." Elsie gives me a pointed look.

"All right."

Once they're out of earshot, Parker scoops me up in his arms, pressing his lips to mine. I pull back. "No. None of those smooth moves until you tell me what's going on with you and Ella."

Parker releases me. I didn't want for him to completely let me go, and feel his loss right away when he steps back. "It's nothing like you're thinking. She's actually wanting to try and fix things with you, and thought coming to me would be a good place to start."

My stare is impassive. *My sister wants to fix things with me?* I look up at the sky.

"What are you looking for?" Parker asks.

"I'm checking to see if the moon is blue, because this, if it's true, is a once-in-a-blue-moon-type event."

He shakes his head, chuckling. "Don't be like that, little mouse."

"Like what? She's already had her claws in one of my boyfriends. Perhaps she's trying for number two."

"I wouldn't go for her anyway. She's not my type. It's only you I have eyes for." Parker moves closer, his gaze full of hunger. He wants me, and the feeling's mutual.

"Oh, Parker, you are smooth."

"Ya know, I'm a charmer. The girls love me." He smirks.

I nod. "Yes, they do."

And I think I do, too. I won't be saying that out loud though. That's probably the last thing on his mind. *Love*. Right now, all I know is he's the one who has a titan grip on my heart, and I don't ever want him to let go.

"Think about what I've said. People change." He sounds like he's speaking from experience.

"What's that supposed to mean?"

Parker sighs as if he knows he's opened a can of worms. "Back in high school, I was exactly like those bullies who were picking on your brother. I probably would have picked on him back in those days, and it's not something I'm particularly proud of."

"So what changed?" I ask.

He pulls me into him, and my arms go around his waist. "There was an incident. There was this one guy me and my *gang* back then picked on pretty much every day." Pausing, he inhales deeply before continuing, "Because of our bullying..." he pauses looking up, ". . . he almost committed suicide."

I gasp. "What?"

His grip tightens around me. "Yep. Because of what we'd done he was ready to take his own life. I'd caught him cleaning out his locker and wondered if he was moving schools because of us. I won't lie—I felt like trash watching him pack his things away into his bag. I decided in that moment that I needed to make a change. So I did. I went up to him and said sorry for everything that we had done to him, and that it would never happen again. The boy watched me, he possibly thought it was some kind of joke. After a moment, he started unloading his things back into his locker." Parker clears his throat.

I look up at him. Emotion is tight on his face as unshed tears well in his eyes.

He continues, "I watched him, then asked why he'd been packing up his locker in the first place. He'd said he felt his time was up. He couldn't deal with the bullying at school since he was already getting crap served up to him at home.

"In that moment, my heart shattered, and a tiny shard fell away. I was a monster in his story. He already was living a horrible life, and we were making life worse for him. I stopped him from putting his stuff away and hugged him. I cried. I didn't care who saw me. The big boy on campus crying with the one he picked on. I didn't care for any of it. In that moment, everything in my universe altered. I promised myself I'd never be like that to anyone again." He quickly swipes the tear off his cheek.

I take a deep breath, taking hold of Parker's face. "You're a good man, Parker."

He shakes his head. "I was the monster in that boy's story. To this day, I don't forgive myself. He may have forgiven me, but I'm not sure I ever will."

I lay my head on his chest and tighten my grip on him. "You saw your mistake, and you changed. That's all that matters."

"I know. I'm still scared that he'll do it. It won't be because of me, but it might be because of someone else. Every week I message him and see how he's doing."

Lifting my head I gaze up at him. Saddened eyes look back at me. "You're a good person; don't ever think otherwise. Not many bullies these days would do what you did. They never own up to their mistakes. You're the bigger person. I'm so glad you still keep in touch with him. Does he live here?"

He shakes his head. "No, he went to Harvard Law School. He's so smart."

"I'm so glad," I say.

Parker buries his face in my neck. I hold him. No words need to be spoken. My touch is the comfort he needs.

A moment later, he steps back. "Let's go enjoy this party and talk about your sister later. Just know there's nothing going on between us."

I trust him. "Okay, but now I can't say I'm much in the mood to party." A cheeky grin plays on my lips.

Parker yanks me back against his hard body. "Don't tempt me, little mouse, or I'll take you right here on the grass." The promise in his words sends a thrill through me. Every inch of me craves him.

"Do it," I whisper, rubbing my body against his, teasing him.

He hisses. Desire radiates from his eyes. His mouth comes down on my neck, and I cling to him as he nips at my skin. My head falls back, allowing him access, and as he goes, he leaves goose bumps in his wake. Slowly, his kisses make their way to my lips, only they're not gentle anymore. He devours my mouth like his survival depends upon it.

"Addison, you make me..." He trails off and doesn't say anything more. Instead, he presses against me, and I know exactly what he means. "Give me a moment to settle down, and we'll go inside for a little while, then I'm taking you back to my room."

"I look forward to it." I give him one last peck and step away, allowing him to *settle*.

At about two a.m. we decided it was time to call it quits. Elsie was totaled, and Willow and Jane had already departed, which left me to get Elsie home. Parker wasn't too thrilled since he was looking forward to a little special treatment time.

"Can't we just put her in a cab and send her on her way?" he jokes. I slap his arm playfully. Thankfully, I stopped drinking the moment we arrived. Elsie doesn't usually get wasted like this. She's at that point where she can hardly stand upright.

"No, something's up, this isn't her. I'm not sure. I have to get her home."

We stand outside in the crisp morning air. Music is still blaring inside, a lot lower in volume than it was when we first arrived.

"I like you, Parker," Elsie yells stumbling toward him. "Most men are jerks. I only ever find that type. Jerk." Her words are slow. *If this is over a guy, it must be someone she really likes.*

"I'm glad you like me." Parker hooks his arm around

her waist, steadying her. Turning to me, he asks, "Will you be right to get her home? You know, with your arm like that?"

"Yeah, I'll be right. We'll get the cab to the front of campus, and I'll use my good side to help her. Now, I have to hope she holds her puking off until we get home." I laugh nervously.

Damn, I really hope she isn't sick in the cab. I don't want to be stuck cleaning up the car. I cross everything and hope for the best.

Parker moves closer. "Tomorrow night. Me and you."

My body sizzles with the promise held in his words. I plan to make Elsie feel terrible tomorrow for making me end my night alone instead of in Parker's bedroom.

CHAPTER
Twenty Two

After surviving work on little to no sleep, I get back to the dorm to find Elsie has finally emerged from her bed. Since we got back from the party, she's had her head in the toilet, eventually making her way back to her bed about five-thirty a.m. I stayed up to make sure she survived and didn't need anything. Needless to say, I suffered at work.

I glance at my watch. It reads 2:30 p.m.

"Good to see you back in the land of the living," I say to Elsie, dumping my bag on the table. I turn to her, and she hunches over, slowly making her way back to her bed.

"Oh, Addison, I'm so sorry about last night. I'm not sure what happened. I was having fun with the girls and a group of guys we didn't know. I liked one of them, and I thought he liked me. Then I saw him humping the slut Stacey in the corner. I mean... in... the... corner... *of the house,*" she cries, and says the last part faster than the rest. She's more than a little outraged by it.

"Elsie, it's not like you to get attached to a guy that quick." I follow her back to the room, helping her to bed. A bucket still sits next to her with a bottle of water on the bedside table.

"I know. I'm not sure what came over me. I guess I'm just sick of Stacey tainting all the good guys at college. Why can't I meet a nice guy? You have Parker, and now I'm sure you're going to stop doing things with me to be with him."

I tilt my head and give her a deadpan stare. *Is she really starting with the 'hoes before bros' thing?*

"Don't start this. You know me. I even gave up a night of passion to bring you home and make sure you survived." She gives me her puppy-dog look. "Nope. Don't give me that face," I say, shaking my head.

"I think I just had a bad night and everything got to me. Sorry."

I sit down on my bed, facing her. "Don't worry about it. For all I know, this thing with Parker may not even last. It's still very early days."

Panic seizes me at the thought of not being with Parker. He's different.

I don't say that to Elsie, though. She's a little unstable at the moment, and all of her emotions seem amplified.

"I see you and Parker together for a long time. The way he looks at you is heart-stopping. I'll find that one day." Elsie sounds drowsy, and I know she needs to rest.

"I'm going to get ready. I'll be out tonight. If you need anything, message or call me. Rest up."

She mumbles something incoherent.

My phone vibrates in my pocket. Opening it, a smile lights my face.

Parker: Hey, little mouse, I hope you're ready for our first official date. I'll be there in an hour. Dress casual.

Addison: Are you sure you don't want me in a nice lacy lingerie piece?

I giggle at my response, knowing it will stir him. Within seconds, I have my reply.

Parker: That sounds like a tease, Addison. I may have to strip you down with my teeth.

I'm about to reply when he sends another message. It's a picture. My heart races as I stare with my mouth open at the image of Parker in front of what appears to be a bathroom mirror, snapping a bare-chested shot of himself.

Addison: I may have drooled. LOL

I search for an outfit while I wait for his reply. Picking out a light pink tee and black jeans, I go for simple and casual. I can't say the jeans will be easy for him to access. What pair of jeans are though?

I hop in the shower, getting myself ready for tonight. I want to look my best. I enjoy seeing the desirous grin on his face that makes my stomach do backflips.

A loud knock on the door makes me jump. Quickly, I smear some gloss over my lips and grab my clutch. When I pull the door open, Parker's standing there. His spicy scent tickles my senses as it hits me.

"Hey, little mouse." His eyes roam my body.

"You like?"

He groans. "You have no idea."

"Oh, I think I do." I crave his touch. The moment I think it, he leans in, brushing his lips against mine. The kiss intensifies in seconds. He clings to me, pulling me firmly against his muscular body. His arms crush me against him. Finally, he steps back, still holding my hand, his thumb rubbing circles over my knuckles.

"We need to pause there otherwise we won't be making it anywhere," he says.

I know he's right. It still doesn't stop me pouting. "All right," I say.

"Come on. I have something special planned."

Excitement bubbles through me. Our first official date. Finally.

"By the way, you look sexy tonight. You could have worn a dress… you know… for easy access."

"No, jeans are a good option," I say. I'm happy with my choice.

I climb into his car, and my phone begins to ring. "Are you kidding me?"

"Ignore it." He shrugs.

Looking at the screen, Mom's name is lit up. "Nah, I better get this. It's Mom." Sliding my finger across the screen, I answer it. "Hey, Mom."

"Oh, gosh, honey, I'm so glad I got you." She sounds flustered and upset. She pauses. Something's wrong. Bitterness crawls its way into my bloodstream and puts a bad feeling in the pit of my stomach.

"Mom, what's wrong? Talk to me." The panic can't be hidden from my voice. I look up at Parker. His brow furrows. He sits his hand on my thigh. Not even his touch calms me.

"It's Ella."

"What's wrong with her? I saw her last night, and she appeared fine."

Mom releases a sob, and everything around me shatters. Every ounce of happiness I had within me moments ago floats away on a turbulent breeze. "She's been in an accident. She's in ICU at the hospital. Can you come to the hospital?"

As much as I despise my sister, I would never wish harm to come to her. Perhaps I've wished for her to not be my sister, but never pain or hurt.

"What accident? What happened?" I register Parker's squeeze on my leg and look at him, tears welling in my eyes.

"She's unconscious, they've put her in an induced coma for now. Come to the hospital. Please." My mother's final plea shoots terror through me.

Is my sister dying? This can't be happening. Please. No.

"I'll be there as soon as I can." I disconnect and look at Parker.

"What's happened?" He studies me as the tears fall.

"Take me to the hospital, please. My sister's there…" The words catch in my tightened throat. "She's been in an accident."

Parker says nothing but backs out of the park and heads in the direction of the hospital. His hand takes hold of mine. It's small comfort.

The last things I said to Ella weren't nice. She needs to pull through. Whatever's happened means nothing. She's my blood. My sister. She needs me, and I'll be there.

"She'll be all right," Parker whispers, assuring me.

I'm so glad he's with me tonight.

"I hope so," I breathe.

CHAPTER
Twenty Three

I race through the emergency room doors with Parker not far behind me. I stop at the desk. A young nurse looks up at me and says, "Can I help you?"

"Yes, I'm looking for my sister. Ella James." The words are rushed, and my heart's racing at a million miles an hour. The nurse taps some keys on her computer.

"She came in twenty minutes ago, and she's up in ICU. Only family is allowed in there." She eyes Parker.

"He's my fiancé. So he's coming with me." I don't care if I'm lying. I need to get to my sister and Mom.

The nurse eyes me skeptically. "She's on the third floor, bed 301."

Without another word, we rush to the elevator. Arriving on the floor, we step off and scan the area, looking for a sign pointing us in the right direction. Parker takes my hand and guides me to where we need to go. For a moment I forgot that his mom works here.

We finally arrive at the room. The scene before me causes me to crumple like a piece of paper. Parker pulls me against him, steadying me. Ella's face is colored with bruises, and a bandage is stretched tight across her forehead. Parker guides me into the room. Mom looks up as we step closer.

A sob escapes her lips and tears a hole in my chest. "Oh, Addison. I'm so glad you're here." She pulls me from Parker's arms and into her own, holding me tightly. I cling to her like my life depends on it. I miss Parker's comfort. I release one arm from my mom and seek out Parker's touch. He takes my hand and holds it tightly.

"What happened?" I ask, eyeing Ella over her shoulder. It's daunting, seeing her in this fragile state. Mom releases me and goes back to Ella's bedside. I step back and know Parker's there to catch me. His arm wraps around my waist.

"Umm… she was in a car accident." My mother runs her trembling fingers through her messy hair, which hangs down her back.

"How did it happen?" I ask. I can't bring myself to step near the bed. Those hurtful words I'd said last time I saw her keep me grounded to the spot.

"I'm not sure… There was a drunk driver and he T-boned her through an intersection." She shrugs, and I can see she's more than a little frazzled.

Parker gently guides me to the bed. "I'm going to go find my mom. She's working tonight," he whispers. I want to scream at him not to leave me, but if it means we can get some answers and it'll help, then he should go. I nod.

Mom's head shoots up. "Your mom works here?"

Parker nods. "Yes. She's doing nights this week. She's a doctor."

"Oh, thank you." My mother goes and wraps her arms around his neck. Parker leaves, and Mom and I stand over Ella's bed. It's as if I can hear my mother's pleas, begging for Ella to wake up even though she is perfectly still and quiet standing there.

"Have any of the doctors told you anything?" I ask as I sit on the edge of Ella's bed.

Mom shrugs. "They haven't given me too much information. Just that she's in an induced coma as she has some swelling on the brain. If it goes down, that's a good sign. If not..." another sob rips from her chest.

Oh, my goodness. Ella, you need to wake up. I don't care about anything that's happened between us. We need you to wake up. I'm sorry for everything I said. I'm sorry for the fighting. You need to wake up and be the sister Devon and I need.

Wake the hell up!

"Excuse me, Mrs. James?" A familiar voice catches my attention.

Spinning around, I see Parker standing there with his mother. She gives me a sad smile. Parker comes right to me, wrapping his arm around me again. It's like a security blanket, keeping away all the terrible thoughts that want to invade my mind and take over my very being.

"Yes?" Mom turns on the spot, eyeing Jules.

"I'm Dr. Kent." She grips a folder under her arm, then pulls it out and opens it. "I'm so sorry this has happened. If there's anything I can do, please let me know."

Mom nods. "Thank you," my mother croaks out.

Jules nods, not releasing my mother's grip. My

mother's sadness seeps into my body. I want to take Ella's pain away. No one should ever have to go through what she's going through right now.

Jules stays with Mom for a short time.

After some time, I ask, "Mom, where's Devon and Dad?"

Mom doesn't look away from Ella, she replies. "Dad and I thought it best that Devon not witness Ella in this state. It could set off a reaction."

I'd hate for Devon to witness Ella like this. Parker and I go in search of some coffee and a snacks.

"How are you coping?" Parker asks as we stop at a coffee machine.

Pulling some money from my pocket, I buy some snacks from the machine beside the coffee device. "I'm pretty numb, actually. I keep thinking of all the bad things that have been said between us, and how we need to move on. I'm not even sure why she dislikes me so much. I only hope she'll pull through this so we can talk about it all."

Parker pulls me into his chest, placing a kiss on my forehead. "She will pull through, and I'm sure you both will sort your relationship out."

I stay in his arms, not wanting to leave them. "Sorry about tonight."

"Don't be sorry. This is much more important. We've got plenty of time to go on another date. I don't plan on leaving you anytime soon."

His words make my chest swell. *Could this, our relationship, be the real deal? Is there such a thing as a soul mate, and is Parker mine?*

What a time to be thinking all this.

"Come on, let's get back," Parker says.

With an armful of snacks, sodas, and coffee, we make our way back to Ella's room.

At midnight, Mom tells me to leave. Jules promises to check in on Mom as much as she can. I don't want to leave, but I can hardly keep my eyes open.

Parker drives me back to the basketball house. I don't care; I don't want to leave him. I need his comfort like I need to breathe.

"Come on, little mouse, let's get you to bed." He jumps from his car and comes around to open my door.

"Mmm… bed does sound good." Although, I may be hoping for a different kind of activity than sleep.

Parker pulls me against him. "Oh, little mouse, don't tempt me," he growls.

I hop on my tiptoes and press my lips to his. His tongue slides right in. Desire pulses within me. I want him so bad.

"Let's take this off the street, shall we?" I whisper against his mouth.

"Gladly." He releases me, taking my hand and guiding me into the house and up the stairs. His bedroom is the last door at the end of the hallway. The house is surprisingly quiet for a Saturday night.

"Where is everyone? I thought there would be a party here again?"

"Not tonight. They've taken it to another place. After the clean-up we had to endure today, they didn't want to do it again tomorrow, or should I say, today."

I laugh. "Yeah, that would stop me as well."

"Coach does inspections to make sure we're law-abiding basketball players. Not many coaches do that, but ours likes to make sure his players are doing the right thing."

"Sounds like a good man."

Parker turns the doorknob to his room, and once we're inside, he slams the door and pounces on me. He rakes his hands through my loose hair, pulling my lips to his. My fingers roam under his shirt, gliding along his smooth skin. He steps back and strips off his shirt. He's gorgeous. His hungry eyes watch me. Slowly, I grasp the bottom of my top and pull it over my head.

I hear Parker hiss. "You're beautiful."

He scoops me up in his arms. My legs wrap around his waist. He carries me to the bed, slowly laying me down on my back. His fingers slide up my belly, cupping one breast in his hand and massaging it. I ache for his touch in other places.

Piece by piece, our clothes come off. With each lick, nip, and groan, pure ecstasy pours through my body. He's my heaven on earth, and in those hellish moments, I know he'll be there to pull me out.

This is what love is.

CHAPTER
Twenty Four

I'm in love with Parker. *Oh. My. Goodness.* With every single touch, he ignites a fire within me. I need his touch, his presence, his everything.

Rolling over, Parker lays beside me with his eyes closed. The sun is peeking through his curtains, and while it's shining on him, I drink in his features. His perfectly aligned jaw. His sculpted chest. Everything is faultless, in my eyes anyway.

"What are you staring at, little mouse?" Parker asks, his eyes still closed.

"How do you know I'm staring?" I reach out, running my hand through his messy bed hair.

"Oh I know all," he moans. He grabs me and pulls my body on top of him. His shining blue eyes stare hungrily back into mine. His fingers trace up and down my back. "You're so beautiful, Addison."

My stomach flips. "You're not so bad yourself," I tease.

In one swift movement, Parker has me on my back, his body crushing mine. His mouth claiming every part of me. I pull him harder to my body. I know we can't get any closer than what we already are. My need and want for him is so powerful, so overwhelming. He presses against me, and I quiver with excitement.

"I love you, Addison," he breathes against my mouth.

My heart stops.

Did he really say that?

I freeze. I look into Parker's eyes.

"What?" he asks.

Giving my head a slight shake, I answer, "You did just tell me you loved me, right?" I need to be sure. Perhaps it was a mistake, and he didn't mean to say it.

Parker beams back at me, his smile wide. "I said it, and I meant it. I've loved you since I first locked lips with you all that time ago. Those times I was a jerk, like when I didn't message and said I would, and bringing someone into the café to tease you. I wanted your attention, I was willing to let you think I was the jerk."

The wind is knocked right out of my chest. I feel the wetness in my eyes, and I quickly blink the tears away.

"I love you, too," I choke out, the lump in my throat making it hard for me to speak. A surge of desire bolts through me like an electrical current. I don't get to say anything else before Parker's intoxicating lips are on mine, and the current pulsating between us is nothing like I've ever experienced before. My body throbs with want and begs for Parker's touch everywhere.

I love Parker.

Never did I think love was even possible for me. I've also never felt like this before. It's as though I'm floating on a cloud.

Everything's somewhat perfect. If only Ella wasn't injured.

Parker and I finally emerge from his bed a little before nine. I'd better ring Mom to see how Ella's recuperating. I claim my cell from my bag and hit her number.

Mom's phone rings twice before she answers, "Hey, honey."

"How is she today?" I've gotten right to the point because I need to know if my sister's going to pull through.

"I've just arrived home. Dad's there now. Her swelling has come down significantly overnight. In the next few hours, they'll bring her out of the induced coma."

My heart leaps with joy. Tears fill my eyes. "Oh, Mom, I'm so glad. How's Dev taking all that's happened?"

Mom's silent for a moment. "He's a little out of sorts. He keeps telling Dad, and now me that he has a game of basketball tomorrow with Parker. I hope Parker can still do it, because I think it's the only thing he's focusing on right now."

"I'll check with Parker, and I'll let you know. I'll come to the hospital in about an hour. I want to be there when they wake her up."

Parker comes back in from using the shower. He looks delicious with the water drops falling from his wet hair and his bare chest on display. I want to climb on him again and lavish him.

"All right, honey. Do you think you could ask Parker

to hang with Dev while we go to the hospital? I normally wouldn't ask, but I don't want to stress Devon out any more than he already is."

"I'll ask him and send you a message." I'm not sure how Mom will take the news that I'm here with him. I'm sure she knows I've played around with guys before but I don't want to go into details with her at the moment.

"Thanks, honey. I'll see you in a little while."

We say our goodbyes.

Looking up, I watch as Parker gets dressed. He turns and catches me. "Like what you see?"

I bite my bottom lip, nodding. My smile's wide. He strides over, placing a kiss on my wanting lips.

"I always like what I see with you." I grin.

"I'm taking you to breakfast," he announces as he finishes pulling his shirt over his head.

"Sounds good. Can we stop at the campus so I can change my clothes?" I'm still in the outfit I had on for our date last night, which never happened. I've had a shower and gotten back into them, but I feel a little dirty.

"Sure, no worries. How's Ella?"

"Yeah, good actually. She's going to be woken up in the next few hours. Also, Mom wants to know if you could hang with Devon while my parents and I are at the hospital? He's not coping too well with what's happened. He keeps talking about the game between you and him tomorrow night," I say.

Without any hesitation, Parker replies, "Yes. I'd love to hang with him. I'll prepare him for our little game. So, I'll take you to campus to change and then we can grab some breakfast. Then I'll drop you at the hospital and go get him." He takes my hand and leads me out the bedroom door.

Dane sits at the breakfast bar, placing a spoonful of cereal in his mouth, and when he spots us, he freezes momentarily. Food sits in his mouth.

"You okay, Dane?" I ask cautiously.

He nods, not saying anything.

"You coming to play tomorrow with Devon at the school?"

He nods again.

Parker doesn't wait for a verbal response before saying, "I'll see you later."

I glance over my shoulder, waving to Dane. *That was really weird.* I know he's not much of a talker, but he seemed more bizarre than usual.

"Is he okay?" I ask as Parker opens the door of his car for me.

"Who? Dane?"

"Yeah. Who else would I be talking about?" I giggle.

Parker walks around to his door, jumping in. "He chooses not to say much. It's just who he is."

We head back to campus, and I quickly race up to my dorm to get changed. Parker waits for me out in the parking lot. Opening the door, I find Elsie, Willow, and Jane all sitting on the sofa. Their heads turn to me, and all faces light up with smiles as screams fill the room.

"You did it, didn't you?" Willow asks. I turn to Elsie, who's shaking her head. I know she didn't tell them about my first time with Parker. Now they know because I didn't come home from my date last night.

"Ahh… well, what do you think?" The grin can't be wiped off my face. I'm sure they can tell from that. More screams. "Come on, girls. I've got to get dressed. He's taking me to breakfast."

"I'm so happy for you," Jane says as she hugs me. Her voice is soft and filled with delight.

"Thanks, Jane."

I should tell them about Ella before I leave. I race and get dressed, and when I emerge, I look at them. They're back on the sofa, talking about Jane's upcoming exams. "So girls, I should tell you before you hear it from the gossip queens around the campus…" I pause, and all their attention is now on me. "Ella was in a car accident last night."

Gasps fill the room followed by a million questions. I hold my hands up to stop them.

"She had swelling on her brain. It's come down overnight, and they're going to wake her up today. She should survive."

Elsie is up from her seat, giving me a hug. "I'm glad she'll be okay. I'm here if you need anything."

I swallow the lump that's lodged itself in my throat. "Thanks so much," I breathe against her neck. All the other girls give me hugs, and I tell them I'd better get going, or Parker might drive off without me.

"He'd never do that," Elsie shouts as I'm about to close the door. Those girls keep my spirits high.

I hop back in the car.

"I wondered if you were coming back," he says, a little smile on his face. "I thought I might have scared you off."

Nothing could scare me away from this guy.

He's my man.

Parker's taken me to a small café a few blocks from the hospital. It's a beautiful morning, and I'm with the best company in the world. After we order our meals, I take a sip of my orange juice. Parker simply watches me.

"What are you thinking?" I ask with a smile.

Parker relaxes back into his chair, crossing his arms over his chest. "I'm simply admiring you."

"Aren't you cute?"

He shrugs. I decide to ask a question that I've been thinking about for a while. "So I'm wondering, do you see your dad at all?"

Parker stares at me. What is he thinking? He leans forward, resting his elbows on the table. "I saw him about three years ago. He tried to make himself present in mine and Paislee's lives. I didn't want any part of it. I don't think Paislee was too fazed. She was going through her 'I hate everything' stage. Mom eventually told him we didn't want to see him anymore, and that was that."

"Oh wow. I'm sorry I asked," I say, suddenly wishing I hadn't opened my big mouth.

His hand reaches out, taking mine. "It's okay. I'm not upset by it." He says.

Right then the servers come and place our food on the table. Things go silent between us as we eat our meals.

I have an uneasy feeling swirling in my stomach. "Are you okay?"

His eyes come up and meet mine. He sighs. "I'm sorry, I was thinking about Hayden and how he treated you, and Ella. That guy makes me so angry. Come on, let's go to the hospital and I'll go see Devon." His voice perks up at the mention of seeing my brother. Hopefully, when I see him afterward, everything will be back to normal. I hate the disturbance that's settled between us.

We rise from our seats and make our way to the car.

When we get out the café doors, Parker gently takes my elbow. "Hey, stop for a moment."

I do what he says and turn to face him.

"Don't beat yourself up over the way I reacted. I'm protective, and when I hear those things… well, I don't like hearing them. This isn't your fault. I can see the wheels turning in your beautiful mind. I love you, Addison. Don't ever forget that fact." He cups my cheeks with his hands and leans in, pressing his sweet lips to mine.

All the doubt and unease wash away in an instant.

CHAPTER
Twenty Five

I walk into Ella's room. Dad sits by her bed, holding her hand. "Hey Dad," I say.

He jumps, turning around, and he's out of his seat and wrapping me in his arms within seconds.

"Oh, Addy, I'm so glad you're here." He pauses and keeps holding me. Tears well in my eyes.

Clearing my throat, I step back and turn to Ella, who looks so peaceful lying there. "How is she this morning?"

Dad returns to his seat, and I go to the opposite side of the bed and sit on the edge of it. "She's doing good, they say. I'm praying when she wakes up, she'll be her normal self. They're saying she could have some memory loss or even temporary amnesia."

"Oh, goodness, I hope not. Although, I'll be glad for her to wake up so I know she's all right. I need to hear her speak, or open her eyes."

"I know exactly what you mean," Dad says.

Things fall into a comfortable silence between us.

After about thirty minutes, Mom comes rushing in. "Oh, good. I haven't missed anything?"

"No. We're waiting for them to come in and administer the drug which will wake her up," Dad responds, rising from his seat to give Mom a kiss. He allows her to take his seat by the bed. She does so without hesitation.

"How are you, honey?" she asks, looking my way.

"I'm good."

"Parker's such a lovely boy. You should have seen Devon's face when he saw Parker pull up out the front of the house." A smile touches her lips.

"Yeah, Devon likes him."

"I'm so glad he's got some friends. I always worry about him. He's come so far lately. It's amazing. I love watching him overcome the hurdles he faces on a daily basis."

"I agree."

Just then, Jules walks in, followed by a nurse.

"Shouldn't you be finished?" I ask.

She gives me a warm smile. "I am, but I wanted to come back and do this."

"Thank you," Mom and I say at the same time.

"Now, what will happen is we'll administer a drug that will wake her up. Sometimes it can be an instant thing, or it could take up to a few hours to wake up."

We all nod as we listen to her words. A crisp silence fills the room as Jules gets to work administering the drug.

I stand. Watching. Waiting. Holding my breath.

Seconds pass.

Nothing.

My eyes fall on Mom and Dad. Their expressions are worried. Mom chews her nails while Dad does his best to support her.

Jules comes to my side, taking my hand in hers. I turn toward her. She gives me a soft smile. My stomach is in knots, and the anxiety is making me feel ill.

After what feels like forever, I lean over to Jules. "How long should this actually take?"

She pats my hand in a comforting way. "It's only been fifteen minutes. Give her time. She can probably hear us. Her eyes are unwilling to open yet. All her vitals are fine, and she's not in distress. She'll be fine."

I really wish Parker was here. I need him. He's my rock—someone I know I can honestly depend on.

"Something's happening," Mom whispers excitedly. She takes her hand. "Ella, sweetie, it's Mom. Please, open your eyes if you can. Please." Tears flow down her face. I release Jules's hand and step closer to Ella's bed.

Ella's eyes flicker open. Then shut again.

"Ella, wake up," I beg.

Her eyes spring open. I breathe a sigh of relief. She blinks a few times before her gaze shifts, settling on me. Her bottom lip trembles, and tears fill her eyes.

I sit on her bed, cupping her face in my hands. "Everything will be okay."

Ella's lips move as though she's trying to say something. "Don't speak. Just rest," I reassure her.

All the weight that had been sitting firmly on my shoulders lifts while I watch Ella grip my hand tightly. It's as if every single bit of dislike, distrust, hostility, and unsociable behavior between us has dissipated. I am so glad I have had the opportunity to fix things with her, but today she needs to rest.

Hours after Ella has woken, Parker finally comes to pick me up. It's closer to dinnertime now, I haven't eaten much since our breakfast this morning. Ella didn't have much to say the entire time I visited with her as she faded in and out of sleep.

I climb into Parker's car. He leans over and presses his lips to mine.

"Eww…" A familiar voice comes from the back seat.

Parker and I crack up laughing.

"Hey, Devon. Did you have a good day?" I twist around to look at my brother, who has his hand up covering his eyes.

"You can look now, buddy," Parker says, chuckling.

Devon drops his hands. "Thank goodness. How's Ella?" he asks hesitantly.

"She's awake. She's good," I assure him. He gives me one of his blinding, bright smiles.

"Good. Can we go eat now?"

I love his bluntness—that's Devon.

"Sure can, but Addy chooses," Parker says as he pulls out of the parking lot.

We pick up some pizza and head back to Mom and Dad's place. Parker and Devon listen as I tell them about Ella and all the details. Devon scoots off to the kitchen to get sodas and plates.

"So, my mom was there?" Parker asked.

"Yeah. She did the doctor thing and woke her up. I was glad she was there; she wasn't you though."

Parker places the pizzas on the coffee table, takes my hand, and pulls me against his body. He leans down, his lips smashing against mine. I revel in his sweet taste.

"Oh, come on, you two. Do that somewhere else." Devon's disgusted voice ruins the moment. I turn toward him to find the plates in front of his face.

"Not one for public displays of affection, hey Dev?" Parker laughs.

"No," he says.

"Let's eat," Parker says.

Slowly, Devon peeks around the plate in front of his face. I'm still in Parker's embrace. When Devon thinks the coast is clear of kissing, he drops the plates and helps himself to a slice of pizza.

Parker tightens his grip around me, nuzzling into my neck. "I wish I could have been there for you today. I'm glad Ella's okay, though."

"Thank you. I love you."

"I love you so much more." He peppers kisses on my neck, and I know if Devon wasn't around we'd end up naked.

Instead of going to classes today, I decide to spend the day with my sister. Mom called this morning to let me know she's fully awake and talking. Once Dad got home last night, Parker dropped me back at the dorm where I filled the girls in on what's been happening. Elsie was mad that I didn't call or message her earlier, but I didn't have the chance. I'm sure she'll forgive me. *I could bribe her with new clothes.*

"You going to the hospital?" Elsie asks, walking into our bedroom as I pull a shirt over my head.

"Yeah. It's time to become friends again with my sister. This petty stuff needs to stop."

Elsie sits down on my bed. "Are you all right?"

The tenderness in her voice takes hold of my heart. Turning, I look at her. "I'm better now. Things are starting to look up in my life. No more fighting with my sister is going to be the best outcome possible. Although, it's sad that it took this accident for us to sort our crap out."

"Yeah, that's just silliness. I'm glad it's going to get better now."

"Are you going to come to the little game tonight?"

She looks at me confused. "What game?" She shrugs.

"Oh, Devon and Parker are having a one-on-one game of basketball. You should come." I grab my backpack from my desk, ready to leave.

"Sounds like fun. I'll come."

At the hospital, I make my way to Ella's room. She's been moved to a ward now, which is a great sign.

I enter her room. Mom and her are giggling about something. It's a scene that I don't see very often.

"Hey, you two," I greet them, and they look up at me, smiling.

"Hey," Ella says, a little hesitantly.

"Hello, honey. So good to see you. I thought you'd be at school today?" Mom asks.

I drop my bag onto the chair. "Yeah, I thought I'd come here instead, and see how Ella's doing. You appear to be doing well." I sit on the opposite side of Ella's bed to Mom.

"Oh, excellent," Mom announces happily. "I might head home and grab a shower and freshen up some." She's off the bed, kissing Ella on the forehead, and is out the door within a few seconds.

Silence fills the room, and I'm unsure where to start. Honestly, I don't know what to say. It shouldn't be like this between sisters.

Thankfully, Ella decides to talk first. "I'm sorry for everything."

I open my mouth to respond.

She holds her hand up to stop me. "No, let me finish. I've been a bitch for so long, and we shouldn't be fighting. I don't know what happened to me. I became so caught up in being the cool girl everyone wanted me to be, and somewhere along the way I lost myself and my family."

I take her hand in mine. "Ella, you don't need to explain anything to me. You're my sister. Yes, I'll admit I disliked you there for a while, but no matter what I still love you. I can't hate my only sister. I'm glad we have the chance to sort everything out. Start over as friends?"

She smiles, tears sliding down her cheeks. "Friends."

We both embrace each other.

All the bad blood that was between us washes away with the tears we shed. This moment will stay with me forever.

CHAPTER
Twenty Six

I stayed at the hospital all day until I had to start work at five. On my way back to campus to go to work, I got a text from Parker.

Parker: Hey, little mouse. I'll be in a little later tonight. Devon's asked me to pick him up. I hope things are good with you and Ella. Love you.

Even his messages cause my heart to flutter.

Addison: Can't wait to see you. Love you, too.

I arrive at the café and slip off my bag, putting it under the counter. "Jen," I call. I hear her voice coming from the storeroom, so I make my way there.

"Hey you," she greets. "You know where I'll be."

It's what she does every Monday night—the book work.

"Not a problem. I'll get to work. Do you mind if I grab

something to eat from the fridge?" She never usually has a problem, but I always like to ask.

"Sure, honey, help yourself. You know you can do that. Also, I'm glad everything's turned out well with your sister. Elsie filled me in."

"Thanks. Me too."

Back out front, I grab myself a cinnamon bun and demolish its sugary goodness.

The hours pass so slowly. I guess it's because I'm eager to see Parker. I find myself checking the clock and time seems to only pass in five- or ten-minute intervals each time.

I decide to give the place a good clean and start scrubbing tables, windows, and cleaning fridges.

Jen pops her head out at about eight. "Oh, my goodness, Addison. It's sparkling out here."

I shrug. "We only had one mad rush about an hour ago, since then it's died down a little, so I decided to pass the time cleaning."

"It's great. Since it's quiet tonight, do you want to start packing up earlier? Then you can head off, if you like."

"That would be great. Thanks."

She disappears out back again. *I love this job.*

I start by dragging in the tables and chairs from out front of the café and lining them against the wall, trying to minimize use of my sore hand. The bell rings, alerting me to a customer. "Won't be a minute," I say as I set the last table down. Turning around, my stomach drops.

Hayden stands there with a bottle of something in his hand. I decide to act normal. "Oh, hey, Hayden. How are you?"

"Don't play coy with me, slut." His words slur as he speaks, and when he steps forward, he stumbles slightly.

"Hayden, are you all right?"

"Stop being nice to me. You don't care about me," he yells, causing me to jump back in fright. My heart hammers with fear. *What's wrong with him?*

"I think you need to leave, young man."

I turn my head. Jen comes to my side, folding her arms across her chest.

"You can't tell me what to do," he hisses at her, then takes a mouthful from his bottle.

"You're drunk," I say. "Just leave, Hayden. It'll be better for you to walk away now, instead of making this something it shouldn't be."

"I'm going to call the police," Jen says and goes to the counter to get the phone. Hayden takes his chance to run toward me, and before I can defend myself, he has a solid grip on my arm. I cry out in pain. This grip is tighter than any other time he's held me. If he could, I'm sure he would crush my bones. I look to the ground, trying not to think about the pain in my arm.

"You'll do no such thing," he growls to Jen.

"Please don't hurt me," I beg as fear engulfs every fiber of my being. "Why are you doing this?"

He forcibly turns me around to face him. There's a glazed look in his eyes. "This is your fault. You left me for *him*. You're meant to be mine." He pulls me closer, then presses his lips against mine.

I want to gag. His breath and its aroma are pure alcohol. This isn't the Hayden I knew. The one I knew wouldn't get physical. Verbal and mental abuse, yes, but physical? Definitely not.

"I've called the police," Jen says.

"No," Hayden yells as he alters his grip on the back of

my neck. He holds it almost as tight as he does my arm. With one quick move, he shoves me hard. My face connects with the corner of the table I'd just set down. I scream. My hands fly to my face as my body falls to the ground. I hear the bell ding. Hayden must be making a run for it. Thank God.

"Don't touch her!"

Parker.

I try to sit up. Jen's by my side in an instant. I watch Parker drag Hayden back out the door. He punches him square in the face. Hayden crumbles to the ground, unmoving. I couldn't care less if he's injured. My face throbs. I pull my hands away, and there's blood.

"I'll go get some ice and a cloth," Jen says before racing off. I'm left with tears and blood falling down my cheeks. I'm not sure what I did to deserve this. I think Hayden has some serious issues he needs to sort out.

Parker's back by my side seconds after Jen walks away. "Addison, look at me. Oh, hell, you're bleeding." He moves my hand off my face, and his concerned eyes turn to stone.

"He needs more than one punch, but I'm not about beating him to death. Even though that's exactly what I want to do." Hatred laces his words.

"Don't leave me," I cry, reaching for him. He pulls me into his lap, wrapping me in his arms, placing kisses on my forehead. It's comforting.

Jen's back. "Here. You need to keep this on that wound, and you need to go to the hospital to get checked out. There's a lot of blood."

I look to Parker.

"I'll take her," he says. He lifts himself off the floor,

then helps me up, and Jen assists me on my wobbly legs. He lifts me in his arms while I hold the ice and cloth to my cheek. "Will you be all right with him?" he asks Jen, gesturing toward Hayden who's out cold.

"Yeah, I'll lock the door, and the police shouldn't be too far away. I'll give them your number, Addison, to check in with you about this."

I nod, not wanting to speak. I rest my head on Parker's chest as he takes me slowly to his car.

"Where's Devon?" I ask, panic gripping me.

"He's with Jimmy and Dane. I'll let them know what's happened. Let's go get you checked out. I'm sorry I wasn't here sooner." He places another kiss on my forehead, and I close my eyes, taking in the moment.

"It's not your fault."

"I know. I can't believe he did this though. When he tossed you against the table, I saw red. I wanted him to hurt so damn bad." His grip tightens around me.

"I'm okay, aside from a bump. Everything will be all right."

"I was so scared," he whispers.

"Me too. Just remember I love you."

He places me in his car. "I love you, too."

CHAPTER
Twenty Seven

FIVE WEEKS LATER

The door to the café flies open, and the bell chimes. Looking up, a smile spreads across my face. Parker strolls up to the counter, a sexy half grin greets me. I lean across. He meets me halfway. Our lips connect. That tingle is still present every single time our lips connect.

He's been at practice, and a sheen of sweat covers his half-naked body. He likes to tease me by coming into the café on Monday nights with his shirt off. Every single time, I have a serious urge to climb him like a tree and claim him.

"How's my favorite girl tonight?" He goes and grabs a drink from the fridge, and I push a blueberry muffin toward him. He picks it up, taking a huge bite.

"She's good. I have no brace on my wrist, thanks to your mom giving me the all clear." I wave my brace free hand at him.

Parker chokes on his muffin. "You went and saw Mom?"

I nod giving him a cheeky grin.

"You went without me?"

"That I did." It's been six weeks since getting the brace and punching that dick-bag. Thankfully, he's left Devon alone. I guess it helps that Dane picks my brother up from school almost every day. Those two have become great friends, which makes me happy. Parker and Dane have also been working with Devon on his basketball, even though I believe he doesn't need any help. He's going to go pro one day, I can see it now. Nothing will stop him from achieving great things.

"Well, no holding back tonight, hey?" He wiggles his eyebrows at me. It's not as if it's stopped him, but it has limited him playing a decent game with me. I would shoot some hoops but couldn't actually play.

"You have Devon coming to play, remember? Also, I think we should have a game of two-on-two. Devon and I versus you and Dane." I walk around the front of the counter. Parker leans against the bench. I press my body against his and slowly trace my fingers over his perfect pecs and the six-pack which takes me to that defined V of his.

"Oh, don't do this, little mouse. Stop teasing me."

I can *feel* exactly how much my teasing affects him. Hopping up on my tippy-toes, I lick his lips playfully. His arms encase me, pulling me tightly against him.

"Now, now, you two. Am I going to need a spray bottle to keep you off each other?" Jen laughs as she comes from out the back with her arms full of drinks to stock the fridge.

Parker laughs, quickly releasing me to go help her. "Sorry, Jen."

I'm sure my face is a slight shade of red.

Jen laughs hysterically. "It's not a problem. It's late. But I'm not sure how other customers might feel about you two practically dry-humping on the counter we pass food over."

I cough at her words. I've never heard her so crass.

Parker laughs. "Oh, come on, Jen, people get food and a show. What do you say, Addy?"

My mouth falls open at the interaction between these two.

"Are you two okay?" I laugh.

"We're playing with you, Addison." Jen giggles. "Just stack these drinks in, and you can close up."

She eyes Parker and places the drinks on the floor next to the fridge, giving him a playful wink. *What is it with the older generation and Parker?* My mother still acts weird around him.

"Yeah I figured." Jen smiles as she makes her escape to the back room again to get the paperwork done for the evening.

I go and flip the sign on the door to 'closed.' I turn around. Parker's right in front of me. His hand glides over the spot that only two weeks ago was angry with color, thanks to the black eye Hayden gave me.

Hayden was arrested and charged with aggravated assault, and of course, kicked off the football team. Jase is now the captain. He deserves it. Although he's been a bit of a jerk to Parker and me since he found out we hooked up. He'll get over it, eventually.

I pull my head away from Parker's touch. "Don't remind me of that night by touching it," I say, turning my head away.

Parker leans in, pulls my face back to meet his, and places a light kiss on the spot, but he doesn't say anything. He doesn't need to. In that small gesture, I can see and feel the love he has for me.

"You know I love you, little mouse." His eyes blaze with desire and want.

"I love you, too."

We get back to stocking the fridge.

After we leave the café, we head to the basketball court. As we open the door, there's a lot of chatter and laugher. Dane, Devon, Jimmy, and Elsie are all here.

"What are you doing here?" I ask Elsie, surprised.

She bounces up to me like an Energizer Bunny. "Oh, my goodness, Addy, there's an exchange student here from Australia. How did I not know this?" she screams excitedly. I flinch at the level her voice goes to.

"Oh, who is she?"

"It's not a she—it's a he." She dances on the spot in front of me. I've never seen her this excited about anything. And for her to be at the basketball court at this time of night, she must have been desperate to seek me out.

"Look out, Elsie. He might have a crocodile as a pet," Parker says.

Her eyes bulge out of their sockets at Parker's lame joke.

"Don't listen to him." I nudge her playfully.

Parker takes off to hang with the boys, who are shooting hoops. He stops midway across the court and comes back to me, kissing me so hard that it makes me dizzy. He takes off again, and I'm grinning like a fool. I can't help but admire him. He is, after all, perfection.

Never in my wildest dreams did I think someone like Parker Kent would ever be mine. Someone I truly love. He makes me laugh at the stupidest things, and I couldn't be happier.

My Monday night guy turned into so much more.

Thank you so much for reading Monday Night Guy.
I hope you love Addison and Parker as much as I do.

Turn the page for a look at My Aussie Guy (My Guy series, #2)
available at books2read.com/u/3GA1np

And come join my reader group Lovelock's Flock
facebook.com/groups/742675105787263

MY AUSSIE Guy

MY GUY #2

(My Guy series, #2)

CHAPTER One

Elsie

My goodness, could they be any louder?

Lifting my head from the textbook I'd been studying, I check around for where the rowdy group are located. The library is meant to be quiet—a place where students can source their reference materials, reflect and read in silence. My gaze finally lands on a table where some of the basketball team—Jimmy, Dane, and one other unfamiliar person—are sitting. I'm guessing the new face is the exchange student from Australia we have all heard so much about. I can hear his accent quite clearly from my table across the room.

The noise is disrespectful to the library and everyone wanting to work quietly in here. I shake my head and turn back to Clifton. "Sorry, what were you saying?" I was sure I'd heard him asking me out. Again.

He clears his throat. "Did you want to go out sometime?"

I cringe.

Every week it's the same—he asks me on a date.

Every week it's the same answer—no.

"I'm sorry, Clifton. I have so much work to catch up on, and I'm booked up for tutoring. I don't really have the time." I meet his gaze and watch as his head drops. Guilt pours over me like hot liquid.

"That's okay. Perhaps when you have a little free time." Clifton shuffles his chair closer. Another one of his tactics. I nod, knowing full well that the date he desperately wants won't happen.

Clifton is a nice guy; he's just not my kind of guy.

Loud laughter fills the room again. I furrow my brow. I can't believe these boys.

"Excuse me a moment," I say to Clifton with a sigh. I'm thankful for this escape from him. At least it puts space between us.

I rise from my chair and stalk toward the noise. Their heads turn my way, and a sudden silence falls over their table.

I stop, standing over them with one hand on my hip. "Do you guys not understand that a library is for study and *silence?* You"—I cast my hand over the table, gesturing to them—"are all obviously not doing either."

Dane takes his cap from the table and puts it on his head. "Sorry, Elsie. We got a little carried away." Always the gentleman, that one. He's quick to fix the uncomfortable situations.

"More like a lot carried away. You're really loud, and how is anyone supposed to get any work done with you lot in here?" My eyes land on the new guy. He has dark hair and a perfectly chiseled jaw line with plump red lips. He's delicious.

My focus is trained on the new guy when Dane speaks. "Elsie, have you met Aiden? He's here for this semester."

So that's his name. I shake my head.

Aiden stands and extends his hand. "Nice to meet ya."

Oh, that sexy accent would make any girl swoon.

I take his hand. It's warm, slightly calloused, and he holds mine for longer than necessary. After a short moment, I withdraw it but there's still tingles which Aiden's touch left. Clearing my throat, I say, "Yep, you too. Now, can you all please shut up or leave? Some of us are trying to get work done." I gesture to Clifton across the room. I catch the hooded stare and disgusted look on Clifton's face. *Great, now I've done something to annoy him.*

"*Sure,* you're studying." Jimmy rolls his eyes then focuses behind me. "If looks could kill, I'm sure we'd all be dead right now. Guess your little friend over there doesn't like you talking to us." He lifts his hand and waves to Clifton with a cheesy grin splashed across his face. *Such a stirrer.*

My dagger-like glare falls on him. "What do you know, Jimmy? You're just a moody prick who enjoys annoying people for the hell of it."

Jimmy tips his head. *Smart ass.* "You're welcome." He laughs.

"We're going now. Just have to find the sign-up for tutoring," Dane says, standing from his chair.

"Front desk can show you what to do." I point them in the direction.

"Thanks for ya help." Aiden places his hand on my lower back as he passes behind me. The simple touch electrifies me. I spin toward him and watch him walk away with the guys until they stop at the front desk. His head turns back for a brief moment then faces the front again.

"Wow," I breathe. I cannot wait to tell my best friend, Addison, about him. It's possible she's already met him, considering she's in a relationship with the basketball captain, Parker.

I make my way back to Clifton. How am I supposed to concentrate now after meeting Aiden? The thought of him makes my heart stutter.

After I finish my tutoring classes for the evening, I head over to the basketball court. When I step through the door, my gaze falls on Addison across the court. I race toward her and Parker who stand on the far side of the stadium. "Oh my goodness, Addy, have you met the exchange student?"

I catch her flinch, and her hands go to her ears. All right. Settle down, Elsie, you're over-reacting.

"Oh, yes, Aiden?" she says.

"Why didn't you tell me he was drop-dead delicious? I had a run-in with him, Dane, and Jimmy at the library earlier today. They were being so disruptive." I huff, arms folded over my chest.

Parker nudges me. "Boys will be boys, Els. And look out, Aiden might have a crocodile as a pet." He laughs as he walks away shaking his head.

It takes me a moment to collect my thoughts. I catch Addison smiling like a goof as she watches Parker walk across the basketball court.

I playfully shove her shoulder. "Seriously, girl, you have it bad."

Her attention shifts back to me, and her smile is seriously blinding. "So, this exchange student. What's he like? I haven't had much to do with him." We follow Parker across to where Dane, Jimmy, and Devon are standing.

"Yeah, I don't know. I only met him briefly; seems nice enough."

"I think Parker said he was going to come tonight. Are you going to hang around and watch the game?"

My feet grind to a halt. "Wait. What? Aiden is coming here tonight?"

She nods and keeps walking. It takes a moment for my brain to catch up with what Addison just said.

I race after her. "So, are you planning to stay?" she asks.

Shirtless, sweat-covered guys? Or lonely in my dorm doing homework? This one is a no-brainer. "Yeah, for sure. I've got no plans tonight. Are you playing?" She's such a sporty girl and not afraid to give things a go. I envy that part of her.

Addison shrugs. "I was going to, but I'm happy to watch as well."

"Yeah, I bet you are," I say sarcastically.

She turns and gives me a knowing glance. She's all

about Parker these days. "Oh, shut it, Elsie. One day you'll find a guy and fall head over heels in love. Then, you'll be the one keen to do whatever your lover is doing. Come on. Let's go sit." She hooks her arm with mine, and we make our way to the bleachers and take a seat.

"Oi, what are you doing? You playing or what?" Parker shouts, waving his hand at Addison to try and get her on the court.

"There's no need. You have more than enough." She points to all the boys bouncing the ball and taking shots.

"Yeah, four is a good number," I agree.

"Oh, come on," Parker begs with a huge grin on his face.

Addison shakes her head.

Gee, they're cute. *Snap out of it, Elsie. Your turn is coming.*

"All right, boys, two on two then," Parker says as the door swings open, and I about fall off my chair.

Aiden...

I spy, with my little eye, a shirtless Aiden.

Leaning over to Addison, I say, "Wow. I'd like to have a lick of that man candy."

She gives me a sidelong glance then busts out laughing, drawing the attention of Mr. Mancandy himself. I slap her. "Shut up. Don't draw attention to us."

I watch as Parker, Dane, and Jimmy casually walk up to Aiden while I bounce in my seat. "Oh my goodness, Addison." Excitement rips through me, and I want to throw myself down on the court and say, *"Take me, I'm all yours."*

"Keep your tongue in your mouth, woman," Addison says. I can see her trying to inspect him as he stands there talking to the guys.

Parker turns toward us. "Looks like you're up, Little Mouse. We have another player tonight. He's also on the basketball team."

Addison stands, and I follow. My chest vibrates.

"What if I don't want to play now?" Addison says with a hint of humor.

Before I can stop myself, I say, "I'll play."

All eyes turn on me. Parker cocks an eyebrow, a humorous smirk on his face. Addison's look mirrors his.

What the heck did I just say?

I look between all the shocked faces. A weight rests in my stomach.

Why didn't Parker mention that Aiden was on the team when I brought up the Aussie guy before?

Addison leans over and whispers, "Do you even know how to play?"

I take her arm and pull her across the hall, out of earshot of the guys. "What did I just say? I couldn't play if my life depended on it. I'm not a sports girl like you."

She laughs, shaking her head. "Just say you'll play another time and that you have an assignment to complete." Addison starts to walk away then pauses, looking back over her shoulder at all the guys who are now staring at us. "What has gotten into you? Or should I say, who?" She waggles her eyebrows.

I take a few deep breaths. "Okay, I can do this. Seeing Aiden has me all frazzled, and I hardly know the guy." The bouncing ball startles me as it echoes around the enclosure, and I look toward it. My nerves are jittery, causing me to jump at stupid sounds. Mr. Mancandy is taking shots with the guys. I watch his muscles flex with each move he makes.

"Wipe that drool you have coming from the corner of your mouth," Addison teases.

"I've got to go." She nods, and I take off, heading straight for the exit.

"Leaving so soon, Elsie?" Jimmy shouts.

I could kill him for trying to embarrass me.

I stop and turn toward him. "Yeah, I actually have an assignment that I have to finish. Sorry to disappoint. I'll kick your butt next time." I swear I hear him chuckling as I pull my shoulders back and strut to the door.

As I'm about to walk out, I look over my shoulder. Mr. Mancandy is watching me. He smiles and waves. I turn and attempt to leave, but instead, my forehead collects the doorframe, and I recoil.

"Ow, crap," I curse, putting my hand to my forehead. I race through the door and away from that stupid court. Gosh, I'm such a klutz. My legs carry me as fast as they will take me while my head has a small throb. *Can I crawl away and die now?*

"Hey, are you okay?"

I stop and slowly turn. My breath is coming fast. That voice. *It's him.* He saw the whole damn thing.

"Yes, I'm all good. Thanks for asking." *Act cool, Elsie. Don't embarrass yourself further.* I brush my hand over my already tidy hair and try to feign a chilled persona.

"Elsie, is it?"

I swallow and nod.

"Maybe next time you can join the game. I could give you a few pointers." He steps closer. The air in my lungs evaporates. My eyes fall on his pink lips. I want to lean up and press mine to his.

His voice snaps me out of my trance. "Anyway, I guess

I'll see you around. Just wanted to check you were okay. I saw you hit your head." He points to the same place I whacked the doorframe on his own head. He leans right into me. My chest constricts. I close my eyes to breathe in his closeness. Then, he steps back and turns to leave, and I'm left out of breath.

"I guess I'll see you around, too," I whisper as I watch his bare muscular back strut back the way he came.

Grab your copy of My Aussie Guy
books2read.com/u/mZBGvE.

To keep up to date with what's happening, sign up for my Newsletter
app.mailerlite.com/webforms/landing/w4c9g7

Or join my reader group **Lovelock's Flock**
facebook.com/groups/742675105787263

ALSO BY
Liz Lovelock

Lost Series
The Lost One—Book One
The Missing One—Book Two
Lost Series Boxed Set

Letters in Blood Series
Dear Captor—Book One
With Love—Book Two
Forever Yours—Book Three
Dear Captor Boxed Set

My Guy Series
Monday Night Guy – Book One
My Aussie Guy – Book Two
My Forbidden Guy – Book Three
The Right Guy – Book Four
My Guy Series Complete Boxed Set

The Jilted Series

Something Old – Book One
Something New – Book Two
Something Borrowed – Book Three
Something Blue – Book Four
Something Beautiful – Book Five – A Novella

ABOUT THE
Author

I'm a wife, mother, reader, blogger, and now an author. I'm always busy doing something as I have so much going on, and my three little ones keep me on my toes.

I'm from bright and sunny Queensland, Australia. I have always been a reader. When I was little, I would be up late reading *Garfield* and *Asterix* comic books and also *Footrot Flats*. When I hit high school, they gave us *Tomorrow When the War Began* by John Marsden, and from there my love of books continued to grow.

I keep a notebook and pen beside my bed for when those late-night ideas pop into my head, plus I'm a stationery addict and love pens, notebooks, and, well, anything stationery.

ACKNOWLEDGEMENTS

I'll say sorry first in case I miss anyone. I'd like to thank my editors Lauren Clarke from Lauren Clarke Editing and Kaylene from Swish Design & Editing. Without you ladies, I'd be thoroughly lost; you've pushed me with this one as well. Thanks for all your advice and guidance.

Thank you Virginia Tesi Carey for fitting me in on short notice and polishing up my work to make it squeaky clean. You're awesome!

Special thanks to Tami from Integrity Formatting for helping make my work look beautiful. You do such an amazing job. I love you lady!

To my fantastic team of betas: Amanda, Rachel, Melissa and Di your input is so valuable. Thank you for all your feedback—you're all amazing. And thanks for being patient with me and pushing me to do better.

A huge thank you to Letitia from RBA Designs for designing another perfect cover, and working with me until I was happy. It is everything I wanted it to be. I love it!

Thanks Lindee Robinson. You're photos were perfect for this cover and to the models

Linda from Forword PR and your team, thank you for all your help and support in spreading Monday Night Guy. I appreciate all you've done.

Thank you to Give Me Books for your help with the

release. A MASSIVE thank you to all blogs who participated in the release and cover reveal, and to everyone who shared anything, I truly appreciate it. We authors would be lost without your assistance.

These next mentions are my other halves of the author world. Without their constant support and friendship, I may have given up a long time ago. They're my cyber sisters spread far and wide around Australia and America, so thank you to Jemma Brown aka JB Heller, Felicia Tatum, TL Swan, KE Osborn, Kaylene Osborn and Belle Brooks. These ladies are truly amazing. I'd be lost without our chats.

To Anastasia, your help has been truly amazing. Without you and your input I'd be all over the place.

To my Flock, I love you, girls. Your support is truly nothing short of amazing. I know I have a safe place in my group with you all. Thank you.

And to my readers, I feel blessed to have your continuous support. Thank you.

To my family, my husband, you're truly wonderful. You've never given up on me. You sit and listen when I need to vent out my frustrations, never once complaining about it. I love you. To my three beautiful children, Millie, Cale, and Finn, you all test my patience, but I'm so grateful to have you in my life to love. Families are forever.

CONNECT WITH
Liz online

TikTok
tiktok.com/@lizlovelockauthor

Twitter
twitter.com/LizLovelock

Email
lizlovelockauthor@gmail.com

Website
lizlovelockauthor.com

Facebook
facebook.com/people/Liz-Lovelock-
Author/100008389321975/

Goodreads
goodreads.com/author/show/8268717.Liz_Lovelock

Instagram
instagram.com/lizlovelock/

Or sign up for my **Newsletter**
app.mailerlite.com/webforms/landing/w4c9g7